Dance Me To The End Of Love

Volume 2

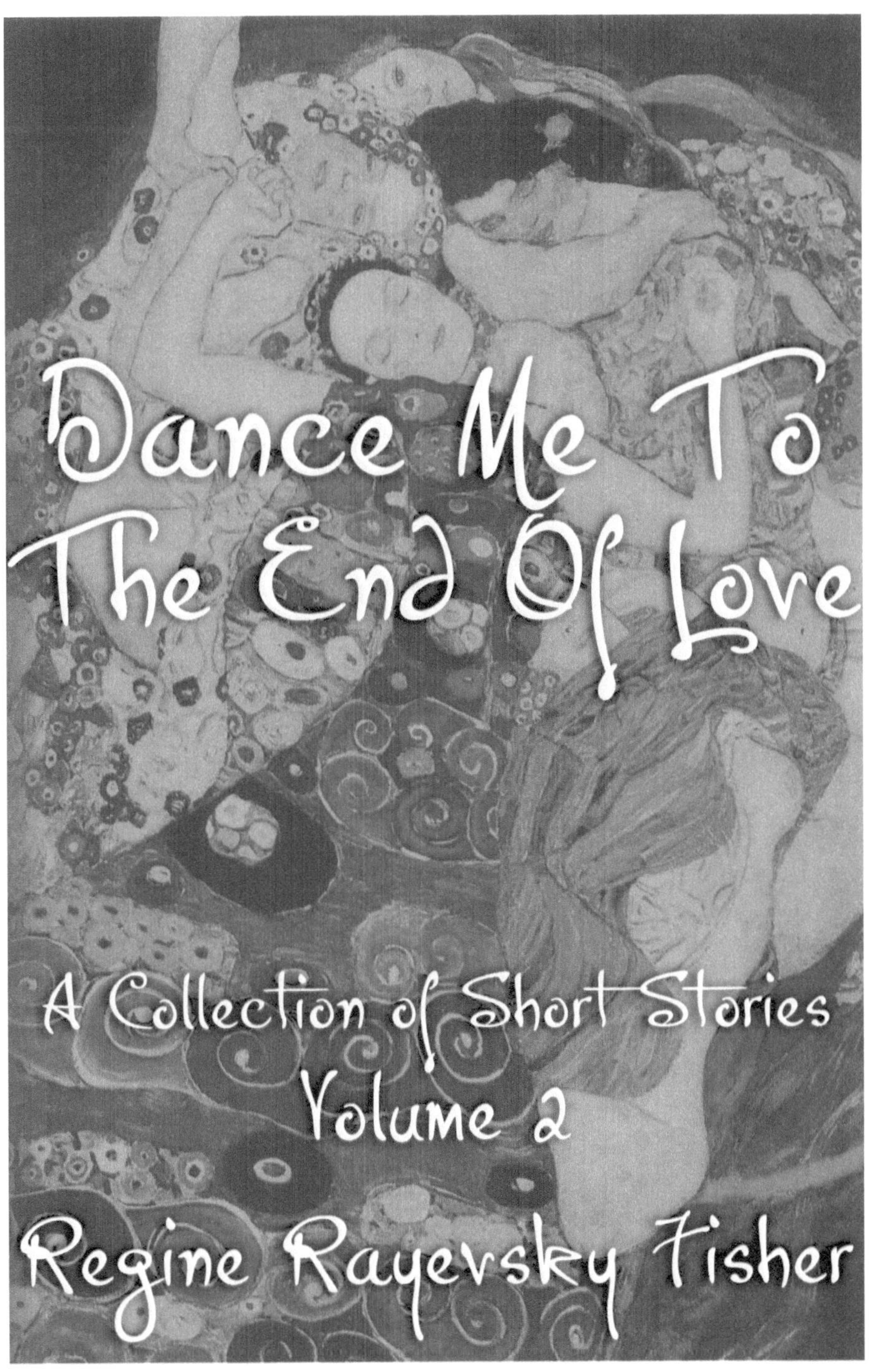

Desert Wind Press

Cover Art
The Virgin, 1913
Gustav Klimt, Austria, 1862-1918
Oil on canvas
In the public domain
Original image is on display at the
National Gallery Prague

Independently published by Desert Wind Press LLC
www.desertwindpress.com

ISBN 978-1-956271-22-5 (paperback)
ISBN 978-1-956271-23-2 (ebook)

Dedication

Waiting for my mother's arrival is my earliest memory. I have asked my mother many times where it took place and described the countryside, myself in a carriage near a lake, my grandmother's face close to mine as she laughs, "Soon Mama will come. Do you hear how the train is coming, how it's bringing your Mama?" And then soon my mother's aroma, as if through a stream of warm air, and an enormous bar of chocolate that had melted in her pocketbook during the long journey to us at the dacha. I am flooded with the memory of her running to the lake holding the chocolate, her familiar face, large white teeth, the puffed sleeves of her dress that fit her figure so well, the taste of the melted chocolate. Where did this all take place, Mama? How old was I? Her answer was the squinting of her eyes she always made when she wanted to remember something, her look into space. She was not sure. But I remember that round blue lake and tall pines and myself in a carriage, though not anything else. Only the moment of joy in waiting for her.

I have always felt myself and my mother and my grandmother and everyone else related to me as parts of each other, and together we comprised a part of something big that had neither form, nor limit, nor end.

Contents

Jesus Came for Dinner

"Moishe, Moishe, what is it? Are you out of your mind? Why do you have this enormous awful cross hanging over your bed?" Moishe was lying down in a hospital bed hooked to various machines by long black wires. His eyes were barely open. His wife Dvoira was towering over him with indignation. He didn't really want to explain anything to her—not that he was in pain, not that he didn't want to die, not that he was scared, not that he was looking for an escape, and not that at the moment he had lost all hope and faith. There had been a knock on the door. Before he could muster "Enter" in a low lifeless voice, the door had opened, and Jesus, as he imagined him, had entered.

"Good evening. Shalom," Jesus said and walked over to the bed on which Moishe had been involuntarily dying, as it seemed to Moishe. He was not ready. He had not had enough time to figure out his earthly journey and all that was related to it. And he did not believe in an afterlife, although he was not absolutely sure.

Jesus approached the bed and sat on it. He observed the tray with food that wasn't touched and asked if he could taste the soup. "It looks really good."

"Please," said Moishe, "be my guest."

Jesus pointed at the spoon on the tray with his own spoon that had appeared out of thin air and said, "Let's share. I start. You follow." Little by little they finished the soup. And then Jesus asked, "What is worrying you, Moishe?"

Moishe looked at Jesus. "What is worrying me? Do you have to ask? Okay. First of all, I don't want to die."

"You won't. What else?" Jesus kindly asked.

"How do you know? You died …"

"And I'm here with you."

"Tell me," Moishe said conspiratorially. "How is it there? What is it there? You understand, we Jews don't believe in an afterlife. But no one really knows, and everyone is dying to know."

Jesus laughed and shrugged, "So when they die, they'll find out."

"Listen, I'm a rabbi, just like you. People come to me with questions to which I don't know the answers. Why don't you help me since you're here? What should I tell people? Is there anything after we die? Or is this it?"

"Moishe," said Jesus quietly, "Can I tell you the truth?"

"Of course," said Moishe. "I'm all ears."

"I don't know."

"What do you mean, you don't know? If you don't know, then who does?" Moishe was getting agitated.

"First tell me. What is *life* according to you?" Jesus clearly was enjoying the conversation.

"Life is the moment of absolute bliss."

"Well," said Jesus, "I may agree with you, but not everyone will. For example, one poet, when asked what life is, said life is a Jewish Street, a ghetto. What would you say about that? Or what was it for the Holocaust victims or the soldiers in Vietnam? Or for the tortured prisoners in Stalin's camps? For famished children, battered wives, for all those with broken hearts?"

Moishe said, "I have no answers. You're the one with answers. Why didn't your father take care of all of this?"

"Ahh," said Jesus slyly. "But who told you that my Father is a caring God? You humans think that you are made in God's image. What if it's not true? What if, on the contrary, God is made in your human image and reflects all human ugliness and cruelty? Did you ever think of it like that? Maybe He sent me here to help humans evolve ethically. Maybe you contaminated God and then came to Him with accusations of 'How could you!' 'After life' is just an invitation to an argument. Listen, your life is here and now. So why don't you enjoy your present? For instance, how about you and I share this wonderfully appetizing apple pie."

"Moishe!" exclaimed Dvoira. "You look so much better. You ate soup and an apple pie. Good God!" Moishe looked at the tray, and indeed the soup and the apple pie were gone. Dvoira touched his cheek. "You ate all of it by yourself?"

"No," said Moishe. "I had company."

"Oh? Who came? Who brought this balloon with the cross?"

"Oh, Dvoira, why do you care if there's a cross or a Star of David?"

"Because I do." Dvoira was indignant. "Because we're Chosen People chosen by God."

"It's a matter of semantics, Dvoira. We're not 'chosen' in the sense that God will bestow favors on us. Rather we're a designated people. Designated to be responsible for others." Moishe breathed heavily.

Dvoira said, "Moishe, first of all, calm down. You've just had surgery. No stress, the doctor said. Second of all, none of it is important right now. You know what is?"

"What?" he said. Dvoira bent down, found his mouth hidden behind the bristles of his mustache and beard and kissed him. Moishe looked at his wife and saw a young and beautiful woman as she had been fifty-five years ago when they met.

At this moment the door opened and followed by his mother, four-year-old Joseph, their grandson, ran in. "Grandpa, Grandpa, I want this balloon." He climbed on the bed and grabbed the balloon. He squeezed it tightly, laughing all the while.

His mother yelled, "Joseph, get off Grandpa's bed! Let go of the balloon!" But it was too late. The balloon did not withstand the pressure from Joseph's little hands – and burst. "You see what you did? Get off this bed." But Joseph crawled next to his grandpa, embraced him, and squinted his eyes from the pure pleasure of being. In his hand a crumpled piece of blue rubber remained.

A Consolation Prize

As was her ritual on the way to her piano lesson, Emma wandered into the most prestigious pastry shop on Gorky Street in the center of Moscow to look at chocolate—crispy magic wrapped in a magnificent gold, silver, pink, blue or green shiny paper that seemed also to produce the sound of a slight whistle that called you to some other voluptuous universe upon the unwrapping. The wondrous waffle stick cost one ruble.

Emma had five that her Mama had been giving her to pay for her private piano lessons that would prepare her for a very difficult admissions examination to the very reputable Gnessin music school. On the rare occasion when Mama accompanied her to the lesson to discuss Emma's progress with the teacher, if her report was brilliant enough, Mama would take her to the coveted store on the way home and buy a silver stick for Emma—never for herself, since money was very tight in their family. Emma would always give Mama a bite to taste the magic, and Mama would acknowledge that it was heavenly. But today Emma was distracted and walked quickly out of the store. Today she would play *Three Fantastic Dances* by Shostakovich. It was a set of miniatures in a style of music that Emma had never heard or played before. Its unusual harmonic features were haunting her. When Emma's teacher had suggested that she give it a try, he added "Dmitrii wrote it at exactly your age, sixteen, when he was still a student at Petrograd Conservatory. He was on the brink of self-discovery." For some reason the teacher had looked at Emma pointedly, and she felt proud. Once at home, Emma had looked at the music sheet and started to figure out how to play it. She got excited —even though it was modeled after traditional dances, Minuet, Waltz, and Polka, the music was exceptionally untraditional and humorous. It was so well crafted, Emma found it easy to lose herself in it. She practiced for hours.

She skipped down Gorky Street—a long stretch from the Byelorussian Train Station to Red Square with its famous red star on Spasskaya Tower, the round clock which sounded every hour for the whole country as if saying "We're not sleeping here, we're watching you." Emma remembered how her teacher had— rather cautiously—handed her that sheet music. "Don't lose it. It's precious. You won't find it in any music store."

"What's the big deal?" Emma had asked her Mama when she had returned home.

"You see," her mother whispered, "Shostakovich is not well liked by the authorities because he tends to step over the line. He's not like everyone else. You will hear it in his music."

And he wasn't. Emma understood that from the first bars of his music that she played. And she had fallen in love with the *Dances*. She had worked hard on them, suspecting that this music was also important for her teacher. Today she would play it for him.

She continued down Gorky Street, glancing at the windows of specialty shops. Nothing new or exciting was displayed there—cheap plastic handbags, scarves with Russian folk designs, unfashionable dresses in gloomy colors, and other uninteresting garbage. All of a sudden, Emma stopped. *Oh my God, it cannot be. My dream. It only happens in fairytales*, she thought. In one of the store windows long up-to-the-elbow black silky gloves were displayed. They shone invitingly as if promising a different life in a different world at a different time. Emma, who had only a school uniform and a dress that her mother had managed to sew for her to wear after school and on Sundays, in her mind was creating all sorts of outfits for herself and her friends. The main attributes of all her creations consistently were long gloves, ones she had seen in an American trophy movie about an opera singer. Everything that the gorgeous actress wore, she wore with long gloves, and they had caught Emma's attention as the main accessory that a woman should have.

In the window next to the gloves was a price-tag—five rubles. Emma's heart started jumping up and down. She thought she might have a heart attack. She walked into the store. There was just one woman ahead of her at the counter, and she was trying on the gloves. They were exactly like the ones in the movie. They promised beauty, success, love, happiness, everything. While the customer was talking to the salesperson, Emma decided on a plan of action: she would pay for the gloves with the five rubles her Mama had given her for the piano lesson, and she would skip the lesson, would call the teacher, and say that she was sick. The plan was perfect and came to her in a matter of seconds.

Emma closed her eyes for a moment and heard the salesperson addressing her. "And you, young lady, what would you like?"

Emma opened her eyes and slowly pronounced, "Gloves." The word had a taste of smooth chocolate in her mouth.

"What gloves?" The salesperson's surprised voice reached Emma's ears.

"Black, silk, long gloves that you display in the window. Here is five rubles." Emma extended her hand with a crumpled five-ruble bill in it.

"Oh, those. Just sold the last pair."

Emma wasn't aware of how long it took to reach her teacher's house. An eternity, a few seconds. She was indifferent to the world around her. As soon as she arrived, she gave her teacher the five rubles and went directly to the piano. She noticed that there was someone else in the room, and usually she did not like to play with another student or another adult present. But this time she felt nothing. The world was unfair, cruel, and as far as she was concerned, if she died tomorrow, she could not care less. As usual she went through her scales and arpeggios, but somehow this time they sounded cleaner and better than ever before. The fear of failure left her. She was at the bottom; the only way out was up. She was not afraid of anything. Next, she played Mozart's Sonata in G to which she applied a different tempo —presto instead of allegro. Previously she thought she would not be able to do it. Her teacher was saying something that she did not hear. She looked at him. He was smiling. "Oh well," she thought, "I must have done something right."

Just before she started playing the *Three Fantastic Dances*, she remembered how in the very beginning her teacher had told her about economy of motion and how to place the thumb in the middle of a white key. Otherwise, it would result in a forward and backward movement that would make piano playing look very difficult instead of effortless. "Put the thumb at about a thirty-degree angle. You gain more control of arm weight, which in turn controls the fingers and the wrist position. Don't swing your elbows. Keep them close to your torso. Shoulders relaxed and down. Practice a lot of arpeggios. Practice octaves by playing Chopin and Debussy. Play octaves with straight fingers. Love it. The music is there. All you have to do is to bring it out."

After the lesson was over, at the front door her teacher said, "It was wonderful. You outdid yourself." The teacher nodded towards the room with the piano where the stranger was sitting. "He loved it. You should be proud of yourself."

"Who is he?" Emma shrugged her shoulders.

"Shostakovich."

When Emma walked out onto the street, a fragment of sun enveloped her whole being in a soft blanket of peace. She slipped into it like a glove.

Across a Campfire

ord, how much has been said about love, how much has been suffered, how many fates have been broken? Once love strangles us, we go off into another dimension, and there is no way to help us unless we can manage to squeeze out of there. Love is always illegal since legality exists for ordinary life. Love transcends ordinary life. Lev Semenych was recalling an excerpt from a story that he had written God knew when. In fact, he had written it ten years before, at the age of nineteen. He was sitting now at a campfire somewhere in the forests near Ryazan—confused, unwashed, in huge leather boots and wearing a sweater of his father's that his mother had kept as a relic. He hated himself as he had been then, the way he had been overexcited over everything on earth, whether it had been a new book, a film, a scientific discovery about which the headlines were screaming, or a well-turned woman's ear that passed him in the metro. He had been a cretin, he thought. Even worse, he had been a cretin in love.

He had been in love with his French teacher at Moscow University, where he had been studying with the literature faculty. Her name was Nadezhda Aleksandrovna, or Nadenka as he called her in his thoughts.

She had a husband, children, a slender waist, and red streaks of hair like his mother's. She smoked cigarettes through a thin, black holder trimmed with gold. In her squinted eyes hid something that evoked a desire to penetrate them, to get to the very bottom of them. Or so it seemed to him.

He wrote a great deal at that time, wrote for her. Wanted to amaze her, shock her. She laughed and once even permitted him to accompany her home. They rode in a cold, empty trolley somewhere far, and when the trolley turned, she leaned against him and clutched onto his overcoat as if she needed support. His flesh burned and trembled under the rough wool of his sweater, and it seemed to him that they were traveling in a carriage somewhere among the clouds and that the earth was far, far away, and no one would ever separate them.

They kissed for a long time in an unknown entryway, holding their breath each time some door slammed. The whole winter passed in this manner. He kept inviting her to his home, and at a certain moment she gave in and went. His mother was not in. Everything happened clumsily, fast, and unnecessarily. But Nadenka kept coming back and coming back, and soon they were both drinking tea with his mother in the kitchen. His mother sharply banged her spoon against her glass and talked of contemporary music, of Schnittke, and how she did not understand his music and did not plan to change her tastes in her old age. Looking straight into Nadya's eyes, she added that everything was going to Tartarus, that everyone had gone out of their minds, and that in general she did not understand anything anymore.

Nadenka was sad on the way home. Brushing snowflakes from her face, she whispered, "Your mother hates me. Despises me. And she's right. I should be at home with my husband and children. But I …"

"She's not talking about that, Nadenka. Not about that," Lev Semenych hotly assured her.

"Then about what?"

"About our life in general, about the country, about Soviet power, about …Oh, you know."

"No, I don't. Lev, I don't want to talk and think about that. My husband's a member of the Party, so please stop making insinuations. They may send us to Paris, you know."

The winter passed, and spring began. Snow on the pavement turned into puddles, and the first daffodils showed their yellow heads. He saw Nadenka more and more rarely. She avoided him. Lev Semenych was shot through with jealousy of her husband who, he was sure, was touching Nadenka's long braids, possibly loved to breathe on the ends of them as he did. And who clearly was calling Nadenka his own.

Then she left. Headed off to Paris. With him, her husband. And her children. Did not even say goodbye. Suffering brought Lev Semenych to scribble an even greater number of pages, some of which made their way to the publishers. And thus it started. They published everything that he was able to write. From time to time it seemed to him that he was a hack, but the current carried him along, and it became impossible to escape it.

Lev Semenych looked across the short tongues of the fire and saw how Nikolai Petrovich, the local forester, was stretching and yawning, then crossing himself on his toothless mouth. Nearby a branch cracked as if someone had stepped on it in the dark, either an animal or a holy spirit.

"Well, I've lived to see the day when I can only chew fish," said Nikolai Petrovich unexpectedly with a smirk in his voice. "God grant that I don't choke on a fish bone; there are so many of them, you can't even count 'em. Scientists count 'em, but who knows what for. You count how many bones in one fish, and another'll have more or less of 'em. Yessir, it's a hopeless task for those scientist fellows." Nikolai Petrovich gathered up his saliva and noisily spat. A bird sang, and a wind blew from the river. The flames of the campfire twitched.

"And just what do you know about scientists, Nikolai Petrovich, that you speak so bitterly of them? You've become angry because you're alone. It's no good being alone in the forest. You should get married," Lev Semenych remarked in a sly, legato voice. The sky slipped over him as if in accord with his point of view, and it seemed as if the stars would fall any moment and start running over him like ants. "They say a wife is a good thing, Nikolai Petrovich. What do you think?" Of course, thought Lev Semenych, it was rather nice on the part of this misanthrope to host him without asking for how long he had come nor why, even to invite him to come fishing with him. Although, of course, this Nikolai Petrovich could become curious as to why a Moscow city slicker had appeared in these Ryazan forests, what he was searching for in a strange land where everything was solemnly quiet and where, it seemed, eternity reigned.

Nature here was a single whole that breathed deeply and regularly. There was nothing to which nature was hurrying. It could not have cared less about time and dates. The twentieth century? Then let it be the twentieth century. The seventies? Then the seventies. And so be it and good. For nature it was all the same. Nature had eternity, and therefore it was calm and beautiful. He who fell into Nature's embrace at first spun like a top from inertia, then began to slow his run, and in the end stopped, fusing into the harmony of the surroundings, even becoming part of them.

Lev Semenych looked at Nikolai Petrovich, wondering whether he had heard the question about marriage. But Nikolai Petrovich either had not accepted the question as being one of those to which one must answer or else for some reason was insulted, and only mumbled something under his nose, got up, and started to descend to the river. After several steps Nikolai Petrovich stopped and looked around. The darkness was all the same to him. Everything here was his. He understood and loved these regions in the heart of Russia. He loved solitude and was glad of his profession of forester, the same profession as that of his father and even of his grandfather under the Tsar. What was Soviet power to him? It did not bother him. Those in power came and went, but the forest remained. Nikolai Petrovich had been born, had grown up, and would die here.

Such silence. Not a soul. Except for the city slicker over there at the campfire who thought that he understood everything in life. A scholar. A writer. But what did he understand, this man who probably kept running to his mother to wipe his nose? The bastard. No, Nikolai Petrovich did not like Lev Semenych. The latter's long nose was not to his taste, his manner of speech was different, too complex. And those whiskers of his. No, obviously a mama's boy. Young, but thinks he knows it all. Why had Nikolai Petrovich bothered with him, promising to show him around, go fishing with him? And now just listen to this quiz kid make judgements about marriage. Only troubling the soul.

In fact Nikolai Petrovich had a wife. She had died, it is true, may she rest in peace. They had lived not badly. Nikolai Petrovich had guarded the forest, while she, Katerina, had taken care of the house. Her name had been beautiful—Katerina. Nikolai Petrovich had never thought about such things before, neither about his wife's name nor about her as existing separate from their home, from the stove where she was constantly busy baking or cooking something, or boiling laundry from the chair he had made for her as a wedding present where she sat knitting long into evenings. She had been a wife who had been near, who had kept his house in order. And then one day she had up and died. No thanks to him for having taken her out of poverty—she had been an orphan fed by some kind people in a nearby village. They had been married in church as she had begged. He had also rewarded her with a civil, legal marriage so that they would have what other folks did. And she did not have to pull out tree stumps but sat in the warmth of the house like a queen. "You're an ungrateful one, Katerina," for some reason stormed Nikolai Petrovich now, and he suddenly noticed that he was standing somewhere far from the campfire, hunched, alone, and that it was cold. He guessed that the river was in front of him, and it seemed to him that souls were flying over it that were laughing at him. *You're a fool, an old fool, Nikolai! What in the world are you doing there? Come to us, you'll get warm.*

It began to drizzle. Nikolai Petrovich turned around and returned to the campfire. Lev Semenych sat at the fire wrapped entirely in a canvas poncho. Only the tip of his beard was showing. "Rain," he complained.

"I'm not responsible for the weather," Nikolai Petrovich answered in an unfriendly tone. "If it's raining, means it's needed—for the leaves there, the grass. Nothing'll happen to you. You won't melt. Of course, it's not like sitting in your apartment in Moscow. We have Nature here. And Nature loves rain."

"Do you?"

"Do I what?" Nikolai Petrovich sat down, ignoring the wetness and showing the city slicker that he was at one with Nature.

"I asked if you love rain."

"What's there to love? Rain like rain. For life it's good, it waters the roots. What's there to love? Is it some kind of woman?" Nikolai Petrovich shivered either from cold or from the rain, but seeing that Lev Semenych was staring at him, opened his mouth and tried to catch one of the drops. "Good rainwater," he said, having caught and swallowed one.

"Do you believe in God, Nikolai Petrovich?" asked Lev Semenych suddenly, carefully taking out a hand from under the poncho and putting it palm down over the fire. "Do you believe in God?" He repeated his question with a hint of mockery in his voice.

Nikolai Petrovich did not like this city fellow who, for hell knows, what reason had appeared here. Perhaps the man was hiding from someone. Maybe he was avoiding paying alimony. Or maybe it was just his nature to arrive, meddle, confuse everything, and then ride off back home laughing. What an obnoxious character. With his hair over his ears like some devil. Didn't even offer to share his poncho and hadn't the foggiest notion that other people get cold and wet like him. You could freeze off your balls here.

Nikolai Petrovich rose to his feet and went to gather branches for the fire, even though they would be wet. Katerina, the devil take her, she was not cold now. He reckoned she was sitting hugging their children Kostya and Polya. He must not think about it nor grieve over it. They had drowned, and God be with them. They were now with their mother. So, God had seen fit to arrange things. How smart they had been, knowing every path around the house, every tree.

As soon as they got up in the morning, they would drink their milk and would run after the birds through the whole forest, and only their heels would be visible. What a misfortune. The day had been hot, and of course, the kids, who were five and six at the time, had taken off their shirts and jumped into the water. Into the river, that is. To swim, to get cool. In the river there was a whirlpool, and they had been sucked into it. Only their shirts remained. Katerina afterwards held the shirts glued to her hands and rocked back and forth in the chair he had made for her. She sat and gazed at the shirts, mumbled something to herself. If you asked her what she was doing, with whom she was talking, she raised her eyes strangely, and they were empty and dark. Then she closed them, rocked back and forth for another day or two, and then she died! She had slipped from the rocking chair like a beanbag. The rocking chair kept moving and would not stop. Nikolai Petrovich had broken the chair into pieces and thrown it out of the house and into the woods so that it would rock no more.

There was nothing to cry about, thought Nikolai Petrovich. It had been willed by God. He would wait until his own hour came and then would join them. He dragged a pair of long branches to the campfire and threw them into the flames. The flames shot up for a moment and illuminated two lonely figures. It stopped drizzling, and for a second it seemed that the night was passing, and it would soon be light. Thank God, thought Nikolai Petrovich. Let it be morning when it will be possible to go fishing and not think about anything.

Lev Semenych pretended he was sleeping. In fact, he was lying wrapped in his canvas poncho thinking how strange human beings were, that things were better for them when they were worse. If people were very comfortable, their souls gnawed at something as if they had grabbed what was not theirs, as if they were thieves. Yes, love was a complicated thing, that was for sure. Lev Semenych took pride in his own wisdom as he recalled again the story he had written. That old man Nikolai Petrovich, that forester—he was probably not old at all, just weathered— and God be with him whatever his age—did not love Lev Semenych. And there was no reason for him to. A dour man, not at all friendly, but it did not matter to Lev Semenych. It was even better this way. This way thought Lev Semenych, I am more alone with myself and with God. Who, after all, will forgive and understand a man other than a man himself and God, God who knows all and sees all? The question is— however—does He see and know everything in advance or after the fact? Because if in advance …The devil take it, he thought, I've started to talk like an illiterate, like that harmful peasant Nikolai who has never been beyond the boundaries of his forest and doesn't even suspect that there are other lives, other countries, cities like Madrid, London, Paris— Something again pricked Lev Semenych's heart, and he felt sick to his stomach and did not have the strength to breathe.

No, no, no! The peasant was right. There was no Paris, and there would be no Paris. There was no Paris where cars flew past with crazy drivers who did not notice anything around them. Lord! Paris had disappeared together with Nadya and with his mother. Again, he was searching for who was guilty when the guilt was his. He had not noticed the yellow light and had driven through it, thinking that at last he had arrived in Paris where Nadya was, Nadenka, Nadezhda Aleksandrovna, whom he had not seen for almost ten years and who was now nearby breathing the same air as he. He was thinking that he had found her address and telephone at last and would soon see her and would embrace her as in the past. It had not been important that her voice over the telephone had been somehow flat, as if it was not hers at all. "Yes, I remember. Lev Semenych. Of course. Moscow University. It's been a long time. A published writer? Really? That's wonderful. No, forgive me, but I don't have much time for books. Today? No, I'm busy, I have an important meeting. Tomorrow? It's possible, but not for a long time. Call me." And that was all. Click, then emptiness over the receiver. But tomorrow, tomorrow he would see her. He drove through the yellow light. That yellow light had been so bright as if it were the blinding sun itself, and it had been possible only vaguely to distinguish that it was not the sun but an overhead lamp in a surgical operating room, and that people in masks were looking down at him. One of the masks had spoken to another in French, "Of course, he's young with a healthy heart, so he survived. But the mother didn't make it. Died right at the scene of the accident."

After a long, long dream from which he had awakened tormented and with aches somewhere in his body, his brain had started to work fast: Where's mother? She was next to me in the car, so excited, so young. First time abroad. In Paris! Everything was so interesting to her: The Champs-Elysees, Montmartre, the Louvre. "Can it be true," she had bubbled, "that I will see real Renoirs, Van Goghs, and all, all my Impressionist friends?"

"Why, you've seen them in the Hermitage and in the Pushkin Museum."

"Yes, of course, Levochka my son, that's true. *But not in Paris.* Here everything is different. To understand an artist completely, it's necessary to be at least a little bit in his skin, to eat from his bowl, to drink what it was that quenched his thirst. To breathe the same air. It seems to me I've already begun to understand French art, music, and literature better. Perhaps it's only an illusion. But how magnificent Paris is!"

"Excusez-moi." A nurse in a white robe and with wrinkles around her eyes had pursed her lips together. "Don't shiver, Monsieur. I'll give you an injection now, you will relax, and everything will be fine. Je regrette beaucoup about your Maman. She had a weak heart; there was nothing to be done."

Murderer. I'm the murderer of my own mother. I killed my mother. Not my mother, but my Mama, my dear, red-haired Mama—not dyed red but naturally red—with freckles all over her face. She was telling me how she had suffered from those freckles when she was young. Wanted to wash them off but couldn't. And how my father met her as she was, with all those freckles, and took her away to a world where she forgot all about them. Afterwards there wasn't time to look in the mirror—the house, family, work on a magazine, various civic tasks she had to carry out, in between all of which she managed to go to the theater and exhibitions. And then my father died—cancer—and her freckles somehow immediately became invisible, and her face sagged.

I wrote about love because I was a fool. Love doesn't exist and is unnecessary. Only pain comes from it. And God doesn't exist. Because if He did, He would not permit some to die and others to remain. That forester, he's a good example. By whom is he needed? For that matter, who needs me?

Already in a half-sleep, Lev Semenych kept on thinking. The meaning of everything was melting, and other images rushed to cast out the unnecessary things that his tired brain thought up. In his purified dream the interior of a public bathhouse appeared. The room was round, and from the high ceiling showerheads hung with multitudes of little holes in them for the water to flow. No one else was around. Naked and shivering a bit from the cold, Lev Semenych stepped onto the cement floor in the center of the circle, turned on the water, and froze.

From the holes in the showerhead where Lev Semenych was standing, instead of water came a flood of light. From all the other showerheads came darkness, but no sooner did Lev Semenych's gaze fall on a ray of darkness then the darkness turned into light. Soon everything around shone brightly, and his heart was so joyful and light that it was with difficulty that he maintained this state of being. It seemed that his heart would, at any moment, break into little pieces and scatter around the world like the sparks from a campfire.

The real campfire had in fact long ago gone out, which did not matter because those who needed it were now warm. Nikolai Petrovich, having long ago fallen asleep and started snoring, saw a multitude of candles of enormous size that reached to the very sky. Nikolai Petrovich stretched over the candles, but their flames did not burn him, only warmed him with a long-forgotten tenderness coming from his mother's hands.

Neither Lev Semenych nor Nikolai Petrovich sensed how they had rolled towards each other through the extinguished fire and how the one had covered the other with his poncho and how their breathing was coming out in a single stream from the damp earth to the sky that was barely rosy from the first rays of the sun.

Nina Petrovna and the Chinese Man

The train was slowly approaching the platform. Looking at the familiar features of the Moscow Kazan Station, Nina Petrovna thought that perhaps she would succeed in quickly catching a taxi to get home sooner. Thoughts of home, of her little apartment on the sixteenth floor where everything breathed memories of her life, thoughts of how she would again be alone, for a long time and possibly until death, brought her to a sad state of mind, and she decided that in the station she would definitely buy her favorite cream pastries, and if she had to go by metro, it would be no misfortune—she would stay among people a while longer.

Nina Petrovna looked at her *sac de voyage* in which were neatly packed a change of nylon underwear, slippers with pompoms, and a kimono, attributes of her past theatrical life.

She had just buried a friend, also a former actress, with whom so much had been linked! Nina Petrovna could have stayed in Kaluga and remained with the family of the deceased, but she had felt that she was superfluous and unneeded, like a glove forgotten in a checkroom. Although she had nowhere to hurry —her pension money had recently come —she had packed her things and, throwing a raincoat over her dark suit, left the weeping family and gray, inhospitable Kaluga.

Moscow, however, failed to greet her with fanfare or sun. Glancing into a pocket mirror, she understood that the seasons of the year had become irrelevant and, though she had been trying to push the thought away, that autumn had come to herself.

She descended the stairs to the platform with an unexpectedly scraping gait, as if she was being drawn to the earth and could not tear her feet away from it.

The crowd carried her out onto a square just as gray as the sky, as the faces of the people, as her mood. She immediately saw an enormous line for taxis.

"I'll do better to look for my cream pastries," she said to herself. Gray diagonals of raindrops whipped her face and her short-permed hair. Ignoring the weather, she looked around, extending her neck like a goose and squinting her nearsighted eyes. She did not wear eyeglasses, for they would give away her age of 68 years. Given her unmarried status, that was dangerous. She used rouge on her cheeks, eyeshadow on her lids and haircoloring that made her hair look like dry straw. She loved to eat and laughed that, "Men prefer meat, not bones."

By long theatrical habit she could not abandon the idea of being admired and guarded it like a precious stone. And although it had turned out that there was neither a permanent companion nor children in her life (somehow there had not been time), she did not plan to make peace with thoughts of old age. She was an actress, and until death she would conquer hearts and rule the world.

After her friend's funeral, seeing the inconsolable husband and children, and the children's children, she had for the first time thought, "And who will be there to cry when I die?" But being by nature an optimist, she had chased this thought far away into the black hole of bad thoughts. "It is useless to think about worries, it only produces wrinkles," she mused, and stretched her lips and eyes in exercises that, she had been assured, would make her skin smoother.

"Well, no pastries. Either they've all been gobbled up or the vendor didn't even bother to come out in such weather. "Pity," said Nina Petrovna looking around and suddenly noticing that she was standing on the edge of the sidewalk in a puddle, without galoshes, and that from the street through a car window two narrow laughing eyes were watching her.

"Where to?" shouted out the merry driver.

Nina Petrovna was confused for a minute but quickly caught on and, using a conspiratorial tone, asked coquettishly, "Will you drive me to the Sadovoye, dear?"

"Get in."

She hesitated, thinking whether to jump over the puddle or to walk through it as if nothing were there. The smiling driver got out of the car, went up to Nina Petrovna, took from her the *sac de voyage*, and offered his hand. Having jumped over the puddle and gotten into the car, she thought, "What an adventure, for God's sake! Why did he choose me of all people? But then, why not? That midget probably thinks I'm terribly rich. He only comes up to my shoulders. Lord, let him only get me home, and what will be will be."

"Well, are you ready?" said the driver, turning to Nina Petrovna. "We're off then." He pushed on the gas pedal and thought how he was tired of smelly women with groceries who fussed with the exact change. This one looked different.

By his flat yellow face and shiny black hair, Nina Petrovna determined that the driver was Chinese and ageless in the Asian manner.

As they drove, they were silent, and the Chinese man kept smiling. "I would not be surprised," thought Nina Petrovna, "if he is planning to kill me and take all my possessions. These Asians are unpredictable, two-faced. Instead of a real face they wear masks, like us actors. I wonder how much this devil will charge me for the ride. I won't give him more than …" Nina Petrovna suddenly smiled, recognizing as they passed Mayakovsky Square, the Beijing Restaurant, Chekhov Street, the Puppet Theater with its famous clock that played a different tune every hour on the hour. She could hear one now, a children's song. Her inner peace returned, and she thought that, after all, it was good to be home, and as soon as the melody died out behind them, she began to hum one of the arias she used to sing.

Just wants me to know she's here, grinned the Chinese man, showing his teeth more broadly than before.

Music reminded Nina Petrovna how in the orphanage everybody had thought she was insane when she had announced on her last day there that she was choosing a singing career. They were stunned at her guts. Even her hero, her music teacher, had said, "You are crazy, Nina. Without a father or mother, who do you think is going to support you in your whimsy? You'll starve. Look, you're eighteen. All your peers at this age are going to work in a factory. It's wonderful there, among normal people, in a real world. Come out of your fantasy. Do you hear me?"

But Nina Petrovna only dimly understood what was being said, her personality could not tolerate self-deception. She would climb up into an unknown world of blazed streets in pursuit of her inner images. She stormed against her destiny by taking a step into the darkness to finally see the light, and she won. The difficulties of the quest had been lost along the way. Four years later, at twenty-two, she was standing on a stage, showered in the thousands of breaths that her performance had unified.

Locked in traffic, the car moved slowly. Nina Petrovna glanced at the Chinese and thought that this ridiculous creature had never been to a theater or traveled. Perhaps, he had never had a woman. Why was he smiling? What was he so content about? His comical ego bigger than himself. Just look at him! Such an absurd little thing! He probably regarded himself as cute, important, even complex. God, he was simple as black and white. But, really, what did she care?

It seemed as if the road kept going up, and it was most pleasant to ride endlessly, all the time up and to know that her building stood on a hill and her apartment was ever so high on the sixteenth floor. From her window, all of Moscow could be seen, the way it had been visible to Napoleon as he stood on a hill while waiting to receive the keys to the city. "Waiting in vain, the short bastard," thought Nina Petrovna and smiled even more broadly as she recalled Prokofiev's opera, "War and Peace," with herself in the role of Natasha, how in a long white dress she had stood alone in front of the world. The dress was pretty, the music imaginative and challenging, but the story was flat and banal, with that old idea that happiness could be found only in a family.

The Chinese peered straight ahead into the rain, thinking that although he was already fifty, his eyes had not yet failed him, his heart and liver were good, his kidneys too, and generally he was aging with wisdom. He felt like laughing but, silent by habit, he prevented himself.

The car braked sharply and stopped. "We've arrived," announced the Chinese. He declined to take money, saying that he would first help her with her bag upstairs, and then she could pay him. That sounded charmingly suspicious.

On her way to the elevator, passing the concierge whom she usually did not acknowledge, Nina Petrovna suddenly said "Hello." To her own amazement she added, nodding in the direction of the Chinese, "This man is a driver. He brought me home."

"Sure! Sure!" fretted the toothless old woman bundled in dark cloth and breathing heavily as she rose from her chair as if to give a salute.

Having opened the door, Nina Petrovna let the Chinese go in first with her bag, while she stopped in the doorway, unable to decide whether to shut the door or not. She entered the room slowly, leaving the door slightly ajar—"Just in case," she decided.

In the dim light of the rainy day the room seemed enormous, holding as it did a grand piano covered with statuettes, vases, books, music sheets, a sofa covered with shawls, chairs, round tables on which lay the kind of magazines and things that could only belong to a woman— cosmetics, perfume bottles, ribbons.

On one of the walls hung many photographs of Nina Petrovna in various roles on the stages of provincial theaters. She had played both the old and the young, and nothing had frightened her at that time. Life had seemed only to be beginning and everything was in front of her, and thus it remained for a long, long time until finally, one day, everything had reversed and in front lay only horrid old age and death.

No one said anything for some time, and the silence was broken only by the ticking of a grandfather clock. A pendulum swung to and fro on the clock's white face, and life in the apartment seemed to continue only thanks to the ticking.

"Who is this?" abruptly asked the Chinese, pointing to one of the photographs.

"Me," said Nina Petrovna, as she followed his stare to a color portrait of her on her knees in a blue kimono with gold dragons that in turn deepened the gold in her eyes that looked with melancholy from under black bangs. As if fearing something, she added, "A long time ago." Suddenly, pointing to a jar of preserves left on the table, she threw up her hands and said, "Oh, I forgot—I wanted to take this to my friend's family. A friend of mine died in Kaluga —you know, 250 kilometers from Moscow. There isn't any food there, and here I left this strawberry jam on the table. Oh well, I guess …"

"Do you still have the kimono?" asked the Chinese. He was not smiling any longer. He did not know why he suddenly experienced a good deal of nostalgia.

Nina Petrovna perked up. "Of course I have it. Just wait one moment. I'll show it to you." She went to the bag left in the entryway where the door was still slightly open, sat down, and opened the lock. Like a blue cloud the kimono appeared, flying in her hands as she rose. Without taking her eyes from her treasure, she said, "You see? Proof that it's me in the photo." For some reason she felt uncomfortable and looked timidly at the Chinese.

The Chinese instantly felt the urge to embrace this unknown woman and to lose himself in her large, comforting body, in the odor of her strong perfumes, in her world that was inexplicable to him. "Put it on," he said.

Nina Petrovna trembled from surprise. "What do you mean, `Put it on'?"

"Just that. I'll turn around." And doing so he put his head onto his chest and became even smaller and looked like a sick child.

In confusion Nina Petrovna first took off her short black jacket and undid the buttons of her blouse. As if by itself, the blouse eased off, revealing a pink nylon slip and a brassiere sewn to order due to Nina Petrovna's large breast size. Her breasts, half exposed, looked out as if in amazement.

The Chinese pivoted sharply on his heels and stared at Nina Petrovna, who was standing half-undressed without moving, precisely the way she had stood at one time in theater dressing rooms, ready to put on her next costume.

Something was improper in the whole scene and at the same time unbelievably exciting, like a first betrayal or a last chance at love.

The Chinese was the first to avert his eyes. Suddenly he clearly understood that he did not care how this old, drooping woman with lipstick peeling off her parched lips, this woman with powder that had accumulated in the creases of the wrinkles on her cheeks, looked in a kimono. Cursing under his breath that he had once again made a fool of himself, that this idea to get outside of his boring existence, to make contact with someone who lived completely differently from him was idiotic, he asked severely for payment for the trip. When finally Nina Petrovna could move again, she rummaged in her handbag and extended to him a five-ruble note. He quickly took the money without any thought of giving her change and, pushing the door wide open, left the apartment.

In her slip, Nina Petrovna roamed about the room as if blinded, yet seeing everything much too clearly. She picked up a newspaper that was lying on the floor forgotten and unread and put it neatly on the table. She then went to a window and ran a finger over the glass and left a mark on the surface. The mark looked rather threatening, as if a wave of hope had suddenly been crossed out. She stepped over to the piano and opened the dusty lid. Her fingers lay on the keys and did not obey her efforts to produce a sound. Suddenly the piano resounded with a thud as her head fell onto the keyboard. She sat slumped over and thought of nothing.

The windowpane shook from the wind, but she did not hear it and she did not know that the Chinese, who had returned with her change, was looking through the open door at her collapsed figure. In the cold draught of air could be felt the arrival of winter. Suddenly shivering, the Chinese remembered that the puddles on the roads would soon be covered with ice and that the wind would be coming from the east, from China, a land where he had never been and probably would never see. He thought that this woman was not his affair and that in his box of a car he was lucky to be little involved with the world. Leaving the change in the entryway, he backed away.

The wind blew more strongly and shut the door tight.

Innocence Lost

What I remember from that morning was the enormity of the sky. Never before had its vast depth and endless blue attracted me as much. had attracted me as much. I was seduced, plunging inside its mysteriousness, to find out what was really on the other side of my consciousness or unconsciousness. I could have, of course, thrown one leg and then another over the railing of my balcony to satisfy my curiosity. But my curiosity was only theoretical. Literally, I was enjoying sipping my coffee in the morning August sun, listening to the birds. I was thinking that I had known so many variants of myself that I wasn't even sure of my true identity. The different sides of myself had not lasted long. They were just fleeting moments conforming to present situations.

Tasha said, "Anya, I'm pregnant." Her name Tasha was short for Natasha. I liked it.

Considering that I was sixteen years of age and did not have much experience in the matter, I was lost in my ability to assess the situation. So I simply asked, "By who?"

Tasha peered down at her coffee cup, obviously searching for directions within herself. "By your brother, the genius," she blurted out as a joke.

I was not amused and suddenly felt abandoned. My brother Pete was brilliant, naïve, argumentative with quotations from Nietzsche, the top student in our special English-language school in the center of Moscow. "What are you going to do?" I said, feeling the possibility of a heart attack, metaphorically speaking. As I recall, a little rain had started from nowhere and was peeing on us.

Pete walked out onto the balcony with his contagious smile as Tasha was saying,

"Nothing."

Pete considered the word for a moment and repeated after Tasha amusedly, "Nothing. Nothingness. I do declare I hate cemeteries. They are lands of nothingness. Such a waste." He shook his head as if in disbelief of human stupidity and walked off.

"He doesn't know," Tasha said.

"Of course he doesn't know," I almost screamed, "and we should keep it this way. He's only seventeen going on five, the moron."

"I love your apartment," Tasha said dreamily. "Thank you for letting me stay here. It's been fun."

Tasha had been brought in by a friend of mine, and since our parents were away, I let her stay after she lamented that her mother had kicked her out of their house. "I won't be a bother," she had said. "I will do your nails." It was summer vacation from school, and I was happy to have a companion. We formed a close friendship fast. I was melancholy and sheltered; she was upbeat, cheerful, and courageous. She was full of plans and things for us to do every day—so much so as if life was a blink of an eye, and we needed not to waste a minute. It had been a happy month until now. Her confession confused and scared me.

"Shit," I said. "My parents are returning tomorrow, so ..."

"I understand. I had the best month of my life. Pete is adorable, and so are you. It would have been great to become your sister-in-law," Tasha laughed.

The first thing I did when I saw my mother coming through the door was to tell her everything about Tasha.

"Abortion!" my mother said without a moment's hesitation. "Where is she? Let me talk to her."

Tasha did not have any belongings. She made do with what she had been borrowing from me. I looked for her everywhere, but she had disappeared. It was hard to say whether she had just stepped out and would be coming back or whether she had left for good. My favorite t-shirt and jeans were missing. I did not know her address or phone number. I called the friend who had brought her. "How do I know?" she replied. "I met her at another party, and she just dragged along. We were drunk. Everyone was drunk …"

My mother was enraged. "Of course she will be back. Of course she will want to have the child and to marry your idiot of a brother and live with us. The little whore. Don't say anything to Pete. He's about to turn eighteen, so if he finds out, the idiot that he is, he could marry her without your father's and my permission."

My mother and I lived for a couple of months in unspoken fear that Tasha would reappear with a bump in her stomach. Tasha's invisibility was looming over our heads as a dark cloud ready to burst. We jumped at every knock on the door, every ring of the telephone. And then we started to receive anonymous phone calls—no one spoke on the other end but instead, someone breathed heavily. What other choices would she have to make us crazy? I tried to look oblivious but in reality, I was terribly mixed up. My mother kept her cool.

Every time I saw an airplane, I dreamed of faraway countries. Jews had started to emigrate to Israel, the USA, Canada, Australia. My mom thought those people were crazy to run after a mirage in the desert. My dad didn't talk about it. But I was curious about this new development in our country. It seemed exciting.

One evening we were seated on comfortable chairs around the table having a family dinner. Mom was not much of a cook, and there was nothing on the table I had not seen before. Boiled potatoes, chicken thighs, bread, butter, pickled beets, and sour cream. Dad looked happy with his shoes off, Mom looked tense. Pete, with his nose in a book, looked indifferent as usual, and I was thinking of where I would be able to smoke in peace. Mom said, "That's it. Pete and Anya have to go."

"Go where?" Dad took off his glasses.

"To America, where everyone goes. We're Jewish, and Jews are leaving this shithole of a country." Mom pointed her finger at my brother and me. "Look at them. They're young and able. They will make something of themselves in the free world. They go first. We will join later as soon as we can."

I said in disbelief, "No fucking way" meaning *at last!*

Pete, barely getting his nose out of his book, said, "Okay. Everyone needs to be saved. Why not us?"

The next morning Mom got on the phone with her friends, then with friends of her friends and so on. Someone put her in touch with important people who knew how to get things done. And in two months, Pete and I received exit visas. That's how we emigrated.

The official route brought us eventually to New York City where the Jewish organizers smoothed our way by offering advice and money for food and lodging. With calm and ease, our nearly perfect English made it possible to enter New York University. I studied bullshit in the Tisch Division, some art and history of rock n' roll. Pete became a student at the Stern Business School. I quickly felt at home with my new Bohemian friends, and often to amuse them told the story of our emigration from the Soviet Union—'the summer of Tasha,' I called it— how Pete my brother seduced my friend Tasha, got her pregnant, and how my mother got scared that Pete would marry her and decided it would be wiser to throw us out of the Soviet Union. "Nothing political." Everyone laughed.

One day Pete said to me, "You're going to meet my girlfriend tonight. Behave. She's the reason I lost my virginity.

"Get out of here," I said. "You lost it with Tasha."

"No, I didn't," Pete said. "I never liked her that way. She was too old for me—nineteen."

～

From time to time I received letters from a friend of mine in Moscow who kept me au courant about mutual acquaintances and things. In one of her letters she mentioned in passing "Remember Tasha, that behemoth of a girl whom I brought to you one summer? Overdosed." She then continued, "Oh, your show, Brady Bunch, they started to play it on our TV. Imagine that!"

"Damn," I thought, after reading the letter, angry at something I couldn't understand and subsequently deciding to cut this correspondence with the old world. I kept on recounting the story of how we emigrated without ever changing anything. Pete informed me he was transferring uptown to Columbia University – the Philosophy Department.

We were young, we were ruthless, we were noncommittal.

In the Library

solde was sitting at the library desk for hours thinking *I'm forty-eight years old. My fiftieth is approaching at menacing speed. I've written three stories. They have been published. I have no idea how that happened. It just did. And now I'm trying to write the next story, but nothing comes out. Nothing. I guess I've already said everything I wanted to say. I exhausted my brain, my heart, my guts. I cannot find a grain of original thought. I am absolutely empty like an old shoe box. I can't think of anything. Chekhov was forty-four when he died. His legacy was 574 stories, 12 plays, letters, essays, and so on. How did I dare to climb the same ladder, to venture into his territory pretending to be a member of his family. It's so very audacious of me. Not realistic at all. Why am I still sitting here instead of, I don't know, walking outside? The day is fantastically sunny and warm.* She looked out the window. *I am wearing high heels. They are so uncomfortable, hurt even when I sit.*

Isolde noticed a boy of about seventeen or eighteen sitting across from her. His very long nose and crossed eyes were focused on the book he was reading. Occasionally he looked at her and smiled, irritating Isolde to the bone. *What does he want?* She was not in the mood for a curious teenager or anyone else at that moment. She remembered that she needed to call her hairdresser to make an appointment to cut her hair. Then she thought, if she ate another piece of lettuce, she would not fit into any of her clothes. Her eyes accidentally stopped on the smiling face across the desk. She thought, *what is he so happy about? Life is a bitch. Of course, he's so young. Everything is ahead of him. He does not yet understand that tasty food makes you fat, that drinks make you sick, love doesn't exist, sex … Well sex, maybe, is what's left, but even that gets tiresome. Work? I don't know who you are going to be, buddy. Maybe a football player, maybe a salesman, or a scholar, a janitor, or a pilot. I only wish for you to love whatever you choose. Because if you don't, there's not much else. You say family. Family? The most complicated shit in the world. Competition between siblings. Fights for parents' affection. Jealousy. Guilt. Lies, etc. We all know that.*

"Do you have any siblings?" she suddenly addressed the young man across the desk.

He lifted his eyebrows and stared at her. "Are you talking to me?" He put his book down. "No, I'm an only child. What about you?"

She lowered her eyes and sighed. "I have seven. I hate them."

"Do you really?" he half-smiled.

"Well, I don't know, but they get on my nerves with their 'Why didn't you call Mom for two weeks' or 'Are you sure you want a divorce? What about the children?' What the fuck do they care? Is it their business?" Isolde did not notice how she was raising her voice.

"My name is Greg." He extended his hand.

She touched it with her fingers, and to her dismay realized that her nail polish needed to be redone. "Oh fuck, I had a manicure only a few days ago—a waste of time and money. Look at it. I have to get another one. You see, I'm a piano teacher in my spare time. My nails have to be perfect." She didn't know why she was telling all this to a stranger. She was incognito to herself.

Greg said, "Oh, it's going to be all right. You live in Princeton, the best town in the world. You should feel happy."

She wanted to say that to be happy with the world one should be happy with oneself, but instead nodded towards the book he was reading, Nietzsche's *The Will to Power*. "What is it about?"

His eyes shone, and his voice became excited. "I noticed that you were trying to write something. What is it? A novel? A letter? An article? Or …"

She quickly interrupted. "A short story, but I have a problem. It's not coming out of me."

"Oh, then you might be interested in reading Nietzsche. Just as an inspiration. First of all, his prose attacks you and captivates you with his spirit and humor. He pushes your creativity, which is extremely important for a writer and for your own development."

"No such luck for me so far. Of course, I haven't read him." Isolde's anger reached a certain level for which she had a name—*uninvited guest*.

Greg continued not noticing her mood. "When you read Nietzsche, his prose will ignite you, and his thought will mesmerize you. For instance, the idea that contrary to what people think that pleasure and avoidance of pain are the main motivations of people's endeavors, it is actually the allure of power that really inspires them. What do you think about that?!" He looked at her as if she was a little girl and he an all-knowing god. "Will to life—" Greg continued, "according to Schopenhauer is the source of much misery, since it is essentially insatiable. But Nietzsche's 'will to power is different.' It is a force that can be transformed in order to create something beautiful. Like your story, for instance. Nietzsche said, 'Self-mastery, self-transformation – that's what the will to power should be directed at. Your real self lies not deep within you but high above you.'" Isolde listened with her mouth wide open.

At that moment a short skinny woman in a nurse's uniform came up to Greg and said, "Are you okay, honey? Time to go." She picked up his chair that turned out to be wheelchair. Isolde's eyes filled with terror when she saw that Greg's legs ended at the knees. They were stumps wrapped in cloths. The nurse turned the wheelchair around and rolled it to the exit.

Before disappearing through the door, Greg turned his head back, looked at Isolde, and with the exhilaration of youth invited her to smile, stretching his mouth with two fingers of one hand. He waved to her with the other.

Isolde's entire way of being flashed before her eyes. It suddenly felt as if she was sliding down a tall mountain at a high speed. To her chagrin she understood that she had not taken her time to stop, to look, to think, to find challenges, to register reality, to appreciate, to smile. She should have asked for Greg's phone number—he could have become her challenge or she his.

She hunched over the blank piece of paper before her, her thoughts ran in different directions. Then she moved her chair closer to the desk, picked up a pen, and smiled. She knew the name of her next story.

Voice Lessons

Lesson #1

"Please tell me about yourself." Showing her attention to me, the teacher, a middle-aged woman wrapped in a black shawl, shifted her body towards me,. She was sitting on a chair with a straight tall wooden back next to a round table covered with a thick embroidered tablecloth, a perfect background for a white marble hand placed in the middle of the table. The hand was big and held many checks and dollar bills, most likely payments by previous students for their lessons.

"There's not much to tell," I said. "I lost my voice. I know I had it when I was five up until ten and used to entertain my parents' guests, friends, and relatives. At sixteen, I sang for my friends, and they seemed to like it. Then I became busy with other things and stopped singing. Only now, at thirty-five, I try to sing at home just for myself, but I can't. I open my mouth, but no voice comes out. I don't understand where and how it disappeared."

"Sit down, honey. Sit down and listen. I sang in the best opera houses of the world for years. Then recently, a year ago, everything changed. My mother got sick, and I had to stop traveling."

"I'm very sorry," I said.

"Don't be. We Greeks are adjustable to such situations. By the way, my full name is Stephaniola Papandopolous. People called me 'Steph' for a while, but I didn't like it and asked everyone to call me Stephaniola. Can you imagine? This salesperson, a nice girl, asked me if she could call me Stefanie or Stef. She said Stephaniola was too difficult for her. I said 'No, you have to call me by my full name.' She got very angry with me. I kept on smiling and politely canceled the transaction. I was about to buy a gold bracelet that cost a lot of money. She lost the commission. I heard how under her breath she called me bitch. I laughed to her face and left the store. The bracelet wasn't that important."

I said, "Very interesting," thinking she was a nut case.

Then she told me a story about a nurse in the nursing home where her mom presently sojourned. "I taught the woman how she is supposed to take care of my mom when I'm not there, even though I go every day. And if I see that the woman does something wrong, I tell her immediately to correct it. The woman doesn't like my visits, but I'm okay with it and still very polite to her. You see, there is a huge connection between the body and the mind. And my body is very important to me because I am a singer. I don't hold grudges. I don't react. I do what's right."

I was listening to her in bewilderment. There was an open piano near us with all sorts of music scattered on top of it and on the music holder. But she didn't look at it even once. I was still sitting across from her with my mouth slightly open when she said, "That will be fifty dollars. Just leave it there," and pointed to the marble hand. "I hope Saturday is good for you. I'll see you next week."

I put fifty dollars in the menacing marble hand and left. In the car I turned on the holiday music channel. Jingle Bells was playing. It was kind of uplifting, but I was really angry with myself. Obviously, I had been duped by this Papandopolous woman. She was a con man, or rather, a con woman. But the moron, of course, was me just sitting there and listening to her bullshit. I had no intention of ever going back.

However, the next Saturday rolled around and at around 2 p.m., I became agitated. I guessed the reason: my lesson was scheduled for 3 p.m. At 2:30 I was in my car driving towards Riverview Avenue in

Potomac where the crazy lived.

Lesson #2

"I'm glad you're here. Sit down. I will give you another example."

Seeing the marble hand, I dared to interrupt her monologue and said, "Maybe I didn't express myself properly when I called you. I need voice lessons."

"I know," she said excitedly. "So listen. My boyfriend … You know, I'm forty-seven years old but never before had the time for a serious relationship. Performing was my everything. I loved it, and audiences loved me. I was always prepared and ready, never missed even one. Anyway, I met him here about six months ago. He came to do some work on the house. And what do you know? After a few visits, he announced that he was madly in love with me. I'm not stupid. He liked the house. But I thought, why not? He was well-built, charming, young, so I succumbed." She laughed. "I told him there was one condition —he could not smoke, not just in my house but at all. He told me that he would stop. I was so innocent that I believed him."

"So what's wrong?" I asked.

"Nothing. Turned out he was married."

"How did you find out?"

"He told me himself. Said, 'it's not a problem, is it?' I started laughing."

"And?"

"I'm still laughing. And that's why my vocalizing is what it is — beautiful."

I didn't know what to say. My vocalizing was down to zero, but that didn't seem to bother her.

"Okay, honey," Stephaniola said, "it's enough for today. Time for you to go. The next student will show up any moment now."

I was wondering who her next student was, but after I put the money in the hand, she shooed me out.

Lesson #3

The following Saturday, to my deep astonishment, I found myself sitting in the same chair looking at Stephaniola thinking it was not she who was crazy, it was me.

"So, sweetheart, how are you?"

I told her that on the way there a driver in a big car cut in front of me, and I almost had an accident. I opened my window and yelled at him, but he just drove away. I said I felt devastated, and stupid, and I wanted to kill him.

Stephaniola said, "You shouldn't have yelled at him. And the fact that you felt stupid was your own choice. Maybe there was an emergency, maybe his mother was dying. You shouldn't have reacted. You constricted your throat. Do you know the difference between vibrato and a trill? Of course you don't, but we'll get to it. Because I feel that the wall between us is coming down. Great, honey. Today was a good session. See you next Saturday."

I was thinking that if I would not come back, I would miss all the fun. Because I realized that what I was paying for was a very unusual form of entertainment.

Lesson #4

"Come, come, dear," Stephaniola said as I entered the room. "Take off your coat and lie down."

"On the floor?" I asked.

"On the rug. It's clean. I vacuumed it this morning. I do everything myself —clean, cook, make my own dresses, fix my hair. I don't rely on anyone. Okay, now that you're down, just breathe. See how you're breathing with your lower diaphragm, just like a baby. That's how babies breathe when they are born. As we grow, we forget how to breathe properly. We forget many good things. And we have to relearn them."

I was lying down breathing, asking myself if I was a character in a play, the name of which I did not know. Stephaniola finally ordered me to get up and continue breathing in the same manner. She said, "Breathe, but don't think about it." This lasted some minutes. She asked, "How are you?"

"Okay," I said.

Suddenly she said, "Do you want to come to my recital tonight? I will be singing in a Greek Orthodox Church. Come, come, I will leave a pass for you at the entrance."

I did go. There wasn't any pass left for me. I was surprised that I didn't care. I paid thirty-five dollars and entered the church.

What I didn't mention previously was that I worked as an editor for one of the publishing houses that produced textbooks for schools. The work was pretty boring but paid well. I had two kids in private school and a husband who a couple of years back had proclaimed himself an author. He had quit his job as a computer engineer and now was taking care of the kids, cooking nice meals, reading, and writing. From the chapters he allowed me to read, I had my doubts that his book would be the next great American novel, but I was supportive of him. After all, it was the point of view of just one person. I had been trying to be open to new experiences, curbing my judgment of the outside world. Take this Stephaniola person. She actually sang well and on stage appeared to be totally normal. The audience liked her. There was a fury of applause after she delivered each song. Since I was not truly satisfied with my work, from time to time to take my mind off those textbooks, I wrote small articles for the local newspapers. Right at that moment, an idea came to my mind to write a small piece on people having different points of view. Really, why do we judge? And judge we do. We all judge from morning to evening every day. What are those judgments of ours based on? Our culture, upbringing, self-esteem or lack of it, education, psychology, hormones, mood, medications, how often we eat red meat, lies we tell ourselves, envy, sloth, and so on, or all of the above? Judgments—are they good or bad for us, for our health, for our development? I came up only with questions. When you voice your judgments to others, it inevitably gives birth to their making judgments. I got up and left the church.

Lesson #5

"Why didn't you come to the concert, sweetheart?"

"I did."

"I didn't see you."

"I certainly saw you. "

"And?"

"You were great."

"Thank you. So tell me truthfully, do you really want to sing?"

"No," I said, "not really."

"What is your aspiration then?"

"I really would like to become a short story writer, to write about things and people ..."

"Who is stopping you?"

Who is stopping me? I thought. Our time was up. I paid and left. In the car driving back home through a light snowfall, I started humming one of the songs I remembered from my childhood. Eventually I noticed that my voice flowed with ease, reached high and low notes without any difficulties. Wow, I thought, what was that? It was magic, pure magic.

Manhattan

"What a waste of a woman," thought Lyuba and immediately decided to help.

Lyuba had become acquainted with Nelya Turchansky the way she did with everyone, suddenly and forever. That is, if her attentive eye fixed on someone, a woman or a man, then this someone became her prey that she strongly held in her teeth the way a female animal holds its young.

Lyuba considered herself to be an experienced woman—almost forty years old, with a thirteen-year-old son who was kind, responsive, and charmingly fat. Lyuba herself tended to full-figuredness and, opening a mouth full of golden crowns, laughed provocatively, "The more of a good person there is, the better. And the more of a Jewish good person there is, even better." Not that Lyuba was religious or even knew anything about the Jewish religion, but she considered herself without doubt the most Jewish of the whole company of immigrants that surrounded her on 108th Street, not far from the Queens Boulevard that belonged to the big city of New York.

New York, as such, was more of a name or an image that was for the while still blurred. Everyone knew that in New York was Manhattan and that Manhattan offered temptations, luxuries, and horrors. All that was unreachable and, incidentally, unnecessary. Here on 108th everything was significantly simpler. A knowledge of English might not be needed at all. Here everyone was familiar—Monya, Sofa. The food was familiar: sausages, pickles, poppyseed pastries. Here it was good like home, the way it was there, across the ocean, in native Kiev, Odessa, Moscow, without any "American nonsense."

Lyuba did not like "American nonsense," although she would find it difficult to say specifically what it was. Like the others she did not take to English, although she regularly attended English-language courses, tried hard to complete the homework and, having smoked up with cigarettes her only room, shouted at her son, "Have you done your lessons? You just wait, you loafer. Think that without a father you can get away with everything?" Her son had not been giving her any reason for such outbursts and, calmly sucking on a lollipop, tore into his lessons.

Lyuba had men or, as she called them, gentlemen callers. Her son liked them and trying to keep at least one of them around a bit longer, he called each of them "Papa," after which the father of the moment would stop calling and would disappear without a trace. Lyuba did not despair and found a new man quickly.

And so, it was natural that when she learned that Nelya did not have anybody, she threw up her hands. "What a waste of a woman! And what a woman! A beauty just look at her! Graduated from an institute, read a pile of books. And no man! Well, we'll fix this matter quickly. And don't be afraid. I'll find an American for you, a real one. It's true that I don't like their `American nonsense,' but there won't be any with you. You are fine in any language, and in other things. A bit on the skinny side for my taste, but that could be helped."

Nelya Turchansky simultaneously drew back and gave in to Lyuba's almost motherly care. So what that Lyuba was somewhat older and without higher education? She was so responsive and kind. A real friend. Nelya did not have any. She had no one at all here.

Nelya decided to reciprocate the favor of Lyuba's care. "I have an acquaintance named Grisha," she said. "A shoemaker. Does it matter?"

"What?"

"That he's a shoemaker."

"Is he a good man?"

"Oh, wonderful. Giving. Just like you. You're simply born for each other."

From word to deed—they immediately telephoned Grisha and invited him over the next Friday, at the end of the workweek. Why they decided on Friday was incomprehensible. No one, as such, was working. Lyuba was on welfare. Nelya, having lost a job in a bookstore not long before, lived on unemployment compensation, and Grisha was in the midst of buying his own business, a shoe repair shop, with money he had brought from Russia. They all liked Friday, however, and even invited a few neighbors and others. The son was ordered to sit quietly.

〜

"Just look at her," Lyuba said, shining her gold tooth while greeting Nelya, who came somewhat late. "I turn in front of the mirror, I primp, I fix myself up. I am pleased with what I see. I say to myself, `Maybe not a raving beauty like your Elizabeth Taylor, but not bad for all that. And then just look, in comes my gorgeous Nelya!"

The cigarette smoke in the room shook from the laughter. Someone said, "Quit putting yourself down, Lyuba. You're still quite a woman."

"And they take me seriously! I was kidding. Nelya! Come, come over here, sit down at the table. I'll pour you a drink. Your Grisha has already made himself at home here and is over on the couch talking with my son. What a good man. How you guessed well. Eat, eat, don't be afraid. Take some mushrooms and some sausage. For dessert I've bought a Kiev cake. And you won't believe it! It turns out it's Grisha's favorite."

Forks loudly beat against plates, knocked shot glasses against teeth and clinked against each other. They toasted and drank for America, for the wonderful country that had given them, unfortunate Soviet Jewish refugees, a harbor. They drank for the American people, so nice and naive that it took nothing to fool them, such idiots! They argued about everything. The noise became interminable, and it seemed that everything was as it should be to have a roaring good time!

Through the din Lyuba drew Nelya to herself and whispered with onion breath into her ear, "See that one? Sitting at the other end. Go around, say hello. She's been here in America for a long time. An American, you might say. Knows Manhattan like the palm of her hand."

45

Nelya looked to where Lyuba was pointing with her eyes. A woman was sitting there and smoking a pipe. Long black hair concealed her face.

"What about her is so American?" asked Nelya like an idiot.

For this she received Lyuba's penetrating look followed by her hissing, "Don't understand? Hook up with her. She knows Americans. Phoo! Let's go together, since I see that you will not manage to cook the porridge alone."

Nelya got up and followed Lyuba to the other end of the room where the unknown woman was sitting. She did differ from the others—her teeth glistened with unnatural whiteness and evenness.

"Capped," Lyuba proudly informed her afterwards. "American. She had them done here. Know how much it cost?" But she did not say how much it cost to cap teeth.

"So, you're from Moscow?" smiled the unknown woman, drawing a match into her pipe.

"Zinaida, dear," gushed Lyuba, "help out a person. Do you see? What a woman is going to waste! Healthy, intelligent. She can manage in any language."

"Well now," said Zinaida, squinting her eyes and focusing them on her pipe, "it's possible to help."

"So you'll do it? Yes? Oh, how I love you, Zinaida. And I love you, Nelya. And I'm beginning to love your Grisha. Oh, how good!" Lyuba jumped to her feet, brushed off her flowered skirt and shouted to her son, "What are you doing? Turn on some music. We'll dance."

$\sim$

The next morning Lyuba telephoned Nelya and said, "So. Zinaida has arranged everything just as she promised. In Manhattan, incidentally. Here's the telephone number. Call. And say as politely as you can— such and such, that you lost your job, and isn't there an opening? And, you know, do it in a feminine way. Oy, Nelya. Grisha just left. We were at it all night. What a magnificent man! He said he'll come back tomorrow. That's fine. A man needs his freedom, needs to rest. But not for long. Got to get the man while he's hot. Get him with tenderness. I said to him, `Grishulechka, what would you like me to make for you for dinner tomorrow? Something that's your very favorite?' And he said `I don't have any favorite, I eat whatever I'm given.' `Well,' I said `are you homesick for beef stroganoff?' `No,' he said, `I 'm not homesick for it. I just had some the night before last in a Russian restaurant in Brighton Beach.' Such a guy. So honest. My kid had already latched onto him. `So long, Papa,' he said. `Come to us as soon as you can. You're fun.' (He's not just a son, he's a golden son.) Well, now. Nelya, call and go there, make him feel sorry for you. Maybe something will come of it."

Lyuba hung up the phone without saying what might come of it, and Nelya was too shy to ask. So she dialed the number that Lyuba had dictated to her without knowing what to say.

But it all turned out to be easy and simple. The male voice in the receiver told her to take a taxi—he would pay—and to go to Manhattan, to Fifth and 52nd. He said it that way, to Fifth and 52nd, without *avenue* or *street*. "We'll talk there," he added. The language he used was Russian but with a slight accent. Nelya took a taxi and went to the proposed address.

In the beginning everything went beautifully. She was met, and the taxi was paid for, something that Nelya had worried about greatly since the meter showed almost twenty dollars. The man who met her turned out to be of medium height, slim, balding, and with flapping nostrils. Like Rolan Bykov's, thought Nelya, remembering the famous Soviet film star. The stranger's name was Roman, and he gallantly offered his arm.

And so unhurriedly, as never before, Nelya walked around a warm Manhattan illuminated by rare stars. Nelya knew neither where they were going, nor why. And although curiosity somewhere rustled within her, she did not summon up the courage to break the silence with some prosaic question. She felt ashamed, but she did not know of what. Roman stubbornly kept silent, although he smiled with the ends of his thin lips.

They approached a high-rise with a brightly lighted entranceway. A doorman stood in front. "How are you?" Roman greeted him in English. (Nelya already knew that these *how are yous* did not mean anything.) The doorman answered that he was fine and held the door open.

Nelya entered as if in a dream. Roman ushered her into an elevator, pushed a button, and they took off briskly. The elevator came to a stop just as suddenly, and they exited into a small hallway. Roman for a long time was unable to get his key into the lock. He smiled wanly. Nelya's heart was pounding under her chin. However, when at last they went into the room, either her heart stopped, or it left the cage of her breast altogether. She gasped: the room was all lit up with candles burning, each with a tiny separate light that did not illuminate anything around it, that did not penetrate the darkness.

Roman laughed and turned on a lamp. The lights disappeared, and in their place appeared a multiplicity of Nelyas and Romans reflected in the mirrored walls and ceiling. In between the mirrors, by an enormous window, was a white couch. Beyond the window rose Manhattan's noise but in the room it was quiet. With her heels drowning in the fluffy carpet, Nelya timidly approached the couch, sat down, and waited.

What she was waiting for she did not know. Just as she did not know why she was sitting here and what was keeping her there. Shame? In front of what? Of whom? In front of Lyuba, Zinaida, or this Roman? Because of her lack of employment? Because of being an immigrant?

Roman went up to her boldly with a glass in his hand. "Champagne," he nodded towards the glass. "If you don't want it, I'll drink it myself."

He drank it in one gulp, closed his eyes, opened them, and having stared at Nelya, uttered, "So, talk."

Nelya became embarrassed. "I'm looking for a job. I don't know. Perhaps you have something for me?"

"A job? Of course. There are a lot of jobs. I personally have, for example, a gallery. Are you interested in art?"

"Oh, yes. Of course, I ..."

"Too bad I had to close it. Exhibited young artists, wanted to help them out. Well, that's my problem. I have a friend, a jeweler. I can call him tomorrow. I'm sure that he needs someone." Roman moistened his lips with his tongue. "And you're not bad, even if you're from Soviet Russia. Forgive me, but I hate the communists. My parents had to flee after the Revolution. I was born in Paris. Then they came here. I adore New York. Madison, Fifth ...how people gather during the season, towards the middle of December, and go strolling up and down Fifth. Oh, wait. I'll show you now."

With ballet leaps he suddenly flitted from the room and in a second returned for some reason in a fur coat.

"Just touch it," he said excitedly. "Such fur, mink! And the lining? See what a bright red? Silk, damn it, real silk. You should see me as I go along Fifth without buttoning it so that the lining can be seen, and there's not a person who passes by without staring. However," he suddenly took off the fur coat and carefully hung it on the back of a chair, "this fur isn't mine but my brother's, though I have one exactly like it."

Roman sat down next to Nelya, who was unable to utter a word, and touched her skirt. "Cotton? Natural? What great material. And how is it buttoned?"

Nelya not only did not resist, she even helped to undo and to take off her skirt and sat again on the edge of the couch.

"No, no, you lie down," cooed Roman in a motherly way. He deftly lowered Nelya's nylon panties without a single word about them and then was silent for a long time as he greedily stared at Nelya's vagina.

She shut her eyes so as not to look at the mirrored ceiling and thought about how he obviously did not like her panties since he had not praised them, and about how not to get pregnant. She wished with all her soul that he would start his nasty business, but time passed, and he still sat immobile looking into Nelya's depths. Her back became tired.

She shut her eyes so as not to look at the mirrored ceiling and thought about how not to get pregnant, then how he obviously did not like her panties since he had not praised them, and. She wished with all her soul that he would start his nasty business, but time passed, and he still sat immobile looking into Nelya's depths. Her back became tired.

What has he found there? thought Nelya. Not Manhattan. Perhaps he's working on his fear of being swallowed by a vagina, if he has ever read Jung. He's clearly sick. Evidently not everything is in order from a surfeit of sensuality. And suddenly she recalled Zinaida drawing on her pipe. How much does Zinaida charge, it would be interesting to know, for providing such idiots like her, Nelya, to such bastards like this Roman?

When Nelya finally had decided that one of them had fallen asleep, Roman suddenly lightly sprang to his feet and offered her skirt back to her.

"*Vous voyez?*" he said unexpectedly in French. "*Avec moi, vous restez toujours vierge.*"

When they went downstairs, the doorman opened the door and asked whether they needed a taxi and, having received a positive reply, blew his whistle.

"I'll call you," whispered Roman, ushering Nelya into the taxi and placing something into her hand. When Nelya opened her fist, she saw that there was a twenty-dollar bill. Perhaps, thought Nelya, she should get out and ride the subway. But the car was already flying from Manhattan at full speed in the direction of Queens, and she decided to remain. Laughter shook her.

~

The next day she slept for a long time, then went to check in at the unemployment office, then slowly wandered home, with the remains of yesterday's laughter still nearing her throat and emerging in strange sounds.

She was still laughing when late in the evening the telephone rang.

"What's with you? Is this the way a friend behaves? The whole day no answer, no phone call, nothing. How was yesterday? Are we beneath you now? Don't want to talk with old acquaintances?"

It was Lyuba.

"And your Grisha. Didn't come, the scoundrel. The whole evening I waited. Warmed up the meat five times, but he's nowhere to be seen. Not at his place, not at mine. As if he died somewhere on the road. I don't know what to think. Swore last night as God is his witness that he doesn't have anyone, that he will come … Why are you laughing? What's with you? Have you gone out of your mind? Why are you laughing hysterically like a half-wit? Well, I'll say the truth, a woman's going to waste. For no reason, going to waste."

Hanukkah Candles

And what was also unusual was that the sun had not gone down yet, and as far as the eye could see, there were empty streets. Not a sound. The houses proudly gazed at one another, sure of those they kept inside. The only surprise in that boring, monotonous street was an addition that was attached to one of the houses. That addition had been built with the intention of turning it into some sort of business. The goal had never been accomplished because of the zoning code.

The addition had stayed empty for some time until it had been decided to rent it out. In it was a single room with a small window, a bathroom, and a closet where a stove and a refrigerator just fit. Masha's heart sagged when she saw the condition of the vacancy, but the rent was low, and so she had taken it.

She thought that it looked different here now in the middle of the day. But she was not sure it looked "better" and the idea did not form into words, only hung in the air around her head like a light drizzle. She walked up to this barrack-like structure that was now her home.

The front door gave the impression of being locked. But the lock broke, and since she didn't have anything inside that she cared about, she had never gotten around to fixing it. She almost entered, but suddenly her mood changed. She sat on the stoop and stuck her runny nose up into the sun's rays. She sat there alone in the splendor of the day and thought of a letter she had sent home to her brother:

"Have you ever experienced a feeling of standing on the edge of a cliff, ready to jump off? Three quarters of your body hang above the sea, and you feel delightfully light. Your heels are already off the earth, and you move up and down on your toes. The sun blinds your eyes. But suddenly there is a wind, a warm caressing zephyr across your breast, and you fall back onto the top of the cliff. You lose consciousness. Awakening but not yet opening your eyes, you feel a spring in your muscles as if someone had poured life juices into you. You get up and dust off your clothes from dirt, pebbles, sand, then turn your back to the sea and leave. Your bare feet do not feel pain. And you recall that at home is waiting your five-year-old offspring who may already be hungry and wants to continue living. And you do not have the right to refuse him …

"…Day after day Mark and I, we wait for you, search for all of you at the window, remembering all the funny, wonderful things we did together with Mom and Dad and you …Say goodbye to Moscow and come. New York is ready for you. And you should be ready for it. Study English while you are still there, but please, join us SOON! We miss all of you so."

America breathed around her, and yet she knew so little about it. She knew the subway's wide mouth that swallowed her to get to work and bring her back home, and that was her America …She knew McDonald's, America's thrill, near the train station. She and Mark had gone to eat there several times. The food, they thought, was delicious.

She knew that there was much more to America. What she did not know was how and when she would find out about that. It was as if their meeting had not yet occurred. She was not sure whether she had the desire left to bother. Her curiosity seemed to be fading away. She felt like a train set in motion that could not stop for lack of brakes—but that once stopped, might not have the strength to start moving again.

One day at work someone had shown her a copy of New York Magazine and said, "Everything that's going on in town is described here. Just read the pages and choose how you want to spend your weekend." She had leafed through the magazine and put it aside. It had looked like a foreign map to her.

The scenes outside, the place of her work, the street where she and her son lived, the endless advertisements, people everywhere—all felt alien to her, like a play in which she did not have a part.

The trees swayed slowly in the light wind as she watched. To her surprise the weather did not change much in December, it was still kind of warm. And nothing really changed, except that suddenly America was cut into two worlds. One world was in preparation to be redeemed. That world was burning with delight at the approaching birthday of Jesus. People sang in expectation. Christmas! Joy and light, and gifts under the trees. In the Soviet Union they too had trees, but only as symbols of the approaching New Year. She used to love to make the ornaments for them out of shiny paper—stars, little balls, all sorts of animals, and the entire family would participate. The others, mysterious and rebellious keepers of tradition, the Jews, were waiting for Hanukkah, their holiday. That was what her son had told her. "We don't believe in Jesus Christ," he had said. "We believe in God." He had learned this at the Yeshiva school where Masha walked him every morning.

"Hanukkah! What the hell!" she thought, shivering somewhat from the breeze or fever. "I don't even know what it means. Mark, Mark! You're torturing your mother. And what if I die? Who would want you? No one." She nodded in the direction of the houses guarded by Santas. Not them, nor the tradition keepers. She had actually longed to be Jewish, to learn more about the culture of which she knew absolutely nothing. She knew she was a Jew because back home she was reminded of it by not getting a better position, or a friend or colleague would say something like, "Even though you are a Jew, you are a good one." So she wanted to find out what it really meant to be a Jew other than a word in your passport, the word that indicated that you were a second-hand citizen …But not just now. Now, most of all, she longed to be held.

She stretched her legs out and bent down to examine her feet. Swollen. Ugly. Of course she could have worn those awful looking sneakers the Americans were so crazy about. They were all one saw in the subways. She did not have to wear high heels and break her legs …Who would want her with her legs broken? And this swelling was from being up so much. Running, running, running: first to Mark's school, then to the subway where a crowded train would deliver her to the "French-Spanish Book Corporation," her bread and butter …

Books and books surrounded her there. That was what she liked—the smell of books. She even liked the dust that covered them. Occasionally she would take a book from the shelf and blow off the gray ashes from its cover. She would start reading until a voice with the sound of chewing gum cracking against back teeth would shout, "Masha, I've been waiting for that file twenty minutes already! Where is it? Did you get it for me?"

Masha would not say anything; she would just gaze for a long minute at the polyester dress her colleague wore, at her badly cut hair, at the expression of superiority in the woman's wrinkled face since she had worked at the firm maybe all her life, in any event, much longer than herself, and then Masha would go off to get the file. "Stingy in gestures and everything else," she thought of her colleagues. The sound of their voices was like a hive. Their eyes stung her.

She suddenly recalled why she was sitting here on her steps at this odd hour, in the middle of the day, instead of working as she had been five days a week for the last year. She thought of her son for a second, and of how they would now be having fun on Saturdays—the unexpected gift she had been promised this morning would permit that. And then she thought of him, her Boss. She should have felt grateful. She did feel grateful. But the gratefulness glued to her stomach, giving her indigestion. She moaned, watching a few small clouds in the sky floating in no visible direction. She felt the urge to join them.

"Mark, sweetheart! Do I really have to go and buy all these Hanukkah decorations I don't give a damn about? Do I?" Perpetual fatigue fell all over her body. "Why can't you leave me alone, Mark? Why can't everybody leave me alone? It was such a good Soviet tradition to celebrate the New Year, that's all. What is this Christmas, this Hanukkah? People should have one God, if they should have a God. I have a fever, and I have a stomachache …… What is God? Do I have any God?"

She squinted her eyes both from the sun and from the pain. "I'd better quit smoking, it's an expensive habit." And then she thought of her Boss again.

Had she really looked so bad this morning that he had said, "Are you all right, Masha?" His voice was so rich! She glanced at him and then lowered her eyes. "Come and see me in my office," he stated as he passed her desk. She sat on her chair fiddling with her pen for some time not knowing what to do. Then without any concrete decision, as if just following different parts of her body, she let the pen drop on the floor and got up. Still gazing down, she could feel the burning spots on her back from the looks the other employees directed at her.

Worms! Jealous bastards, ignorant idiots raving "Okeydokey" right and left. Even she could do better when she cared to speak this damn English. Her hands were trembling. What language was he going to try? If he knew any Russian, she would show him her level. Well, French would be okay too. Her French was not so bad. She had been a French teacher in her other life. She threw the cigarette into a wastebasket before entering his office.

But when he spoke, it was not a question of language. He was the Boss, and he offered her a cigarette, saying that he felt European. No one understood him. But he was glad that she was in America because it was a great country. He, for example, was enjoying talking to a psychoanalyst and taking dance lessons. "Disco," he said. "Yes, baby, the '70's!" Did she know how to dance disco? She did not.

Then he asked her questions. He was the Boss, and she answered all his questions. She told him about her living with a small child who was studying at a Yeshiva because they took him for free. Her hard time adapting in America after the Soviet Union. Her not having any friends or relatives here in the States …She told him her real last name was Lanskyrovich. But her counselor at the New York Association for New Americans had said the name was too long. So she altered it to Lansky, and beyond that, she said, there was nothing else to tell. After she finished, she felt sick inside.

He was not even the Boss. He was a son of the Boss. He was an S.O.B. She knew enough English to make that out. He did not break the silence for some time. Then he took a few steps to where she was sitting and just stood there, his smile hidden in his thick mustache. So when she rose, her lips touched his by accident. There was no other way around his face. His lips met hers as if they were giving in.

But soon he embraced her, tightly pulling her to his chest, whispering something about his wife growing old and fat. The kids were driving him crazy too with their demands, and this office, his father's venture, was beginning to get on his nerves. He would rather be on the French Riviera. The S.O.B …

His mustache tickled. He told her she could go home and rest. She should take some medicine. He knew of a nice place just a couple of blocks away, where the two of them might find a refuge from their problems. Sometimes, not too often. Because of his visits to a psychoanalyst twice a week and the dance classes. She nearly drowned in the warmth of his arms.

But then she thought, the S.O.B. has a problem with his old, fat wife and with not being on the French Riviera. That was understandable. That was a problem. And he knew a solution. The psychoanalyst and the disco and her. She was a solution too. As some others apparently had been before her, according to the rumors around the floor.

The S.O.B. was oh so generous. His arms finally let her go, and, freeing themselves, they stuck in his pockets. His pockets were deep, she could not see his bare wrists. Only the wool of his richly made suit. A great suit, she thought. He said he would raise her salary by twenty dollars a week.

Tomorrow was Hanukkah, and she remembered that her son had asked her to buy the decorations for it. And where was God to make her feel better? Still, before even taking any medicine, she went to the store and bought everything her son had asked for and more. Because now she felt richer by twenty dollars.

When her son came back home from school that day, he saw the packages stuck in the corner of the room. In his excitement he did not notice that his mother had added things to his list. The things she had added were sold for Christmas, lights, and all. But there was nothing unusual in that. That was the way it always had been back in Moscow, the way without God.

He had his candle holder, given to him at school. He called it a "menorah." He lit his first Hanukkah candle the next evening, at the right time after the sunset. He looked back at his mother. She stood right behind him since she was concerned about his playing with the matches.

Away from the multitude of lights from the colored bulbs and the candle and the cigarette she was squeezing between her fingers at a distance, she must have looked like a shadow except for the eyes. For some reason, her eyes were wet. That was unusual.

The following Friday she received her weekly check for a hundred-twenty-five dollars, plus twenty dollars in cash. Mr. Tawil, the financial officer, an Egyptian who spoke fluent French, gave her the envelope with her allowance. His bald head shone from perspiration as he sat in front of her on a chair away from his desk. He took off his jacket. His sweaty purplish neck showed through his greasy shirt-collar. His mouth smiled, but the rest—the bulk of his body, the black of his Red-cross shoes, the gold of his signet ring—looked menacing. They sat against each other, their knees almost touching. He put his thieving hands on her knee and squeezed them, his chunky short fingers waiting for a response. Masha turned into stone.

"See what I do for you?" Mr. Tawil said. "I go and fight! I humiliate myself in front of the young Boss and beg him to raise your salary. I take chances so that you have some relief. Look here. Cash. See. Twenty dollars, cash! It's a lot of money! Believe me, I know the price of every penny, I have five kids to feed and a wife." As he talked, he caressed her knees with strokes that grew longer and longer. "I don't like women to wear pants," he said suddenly, pressing his thumb in between her legs. "It looks good on you, but I prefer," he pressed his thumb even harder, "a mystery under the skirt …until the skirt goes down." He laughed a thick laugh of a contented man. "Do me a favor, put on a skirt when you see me in private." He giggled.

"We have a date?" Masha asked, her face greenish, perhaps from the shade of his desk lamp.

"Well, we'll go to a motel." He hesitated for a moment. "I would think you would want to …to do something nice for me too, ah?"

"Then, why a skirt, if to a motel?" Masha said, her voice free of any expression.

Doubtful about her mood, he said coolly, "Because I like it that way."

A head with a cascade of black curls appeared through the door.

"Mr. Tawil! There are a lot of us here waiting for our envelopes." There was something possessive in that voice. "We are wasting our time, you know. We have to work." The woman helped herself into the room swinging her considerable bosom from Mr. Tawil to Masha and back.

"You may go, Miss Lansky. I've answered all your questions," Mr.

Tawil said, rising from his chair, his wry face frowning upon Masha's. "Now, dear," he said to the woman …

Masha went back to her table and sat down. "My parents," she thought, "believe that I am a Queen, one who has power over all." She lifted her cold eyes. Everybody was watching her. She remembered that tonight was the eighth day of Hanukkah and Mark would light his last candle. And tomorrow, the young Boss had told her, she should meet him on her lunch hour. He had given her an address and said it was close to work, so she should not worry about being late.

Masha picked up the envelope with the money and took out the bill. Twenty dollars! She drew it closer to her eyes, examining the pictures carefully. The portrait of a man on one side left her doubtful about who that might be, but the house on the other side drew her attention. A curious expression came over her face. She smelled the bill and held it against the light. A fortune! She displayed real pleasure in possessing it. Slowly she placed it in her pocketbook under the torn liner. Then she noisily opened her brown lunch bag brought from home and began to eat.

〜

God, man could be jealous, which is nothing unusual, but it was embarrassing to see Mr. Tawil in his demonic mood: his sexual libido stripped him of rationality. "You were seen with the young Boss!" he raved. "It's the principle of it!" he groaned. "I don't care what you do. But!" He pointed his fat finger at her. "Don't take me for a fool, dear. It is me you owe, sweetie. I pull you out of shit and give you the money! And this is how you repay me?! I will throw you out! You won't last a day. You don't know me. I'll show you how to play games with me …"

And he did. The staff, it was reported discreetly to the old Boss, had gotten impatient with her incompetence. This debut must be over. "Finita la commedia!" Mr. Tawil exclaimed on return to his office. "Justice must prevail."

As to S.O.B., she never saw him after she was fired—except once, during Christmas time five years later, when she and her American husband sat at the table next to his at Le Cirque, a very chic New York establishment. He was lunching with his family, and she was amused to see that his mouth fell open when he recognized her.

Innocence Prevails

The camp bus stopped at Harvard Square. The moment the doors opened, an impatient herd of children kicking each other jumped out anxiously looking for those who were supposed to meet them. John, Sophie's son, humped under his backpack, was among the rambunctious crowd. Sophie ran to grab him and sealed him in her embrace.

"Mom, it was just two weeks! Calm down."

Sophie marveled at the way he said it, obviously he had grown up. Eight years old, almost an adult, she thought.

In the car driving home she asked, "Would you like Chinese for dinner?"

"No," John said.

"Pizza?"

"No."

To Sophie, this sounded so out of the ordinary that she was at a loss for words. An unusual turn of events, she thought and glanced at him. He appeared a bit mysterious. "What's the matter?" Sophie asked. John did not answer. "Listen," Sophie started. "I understand you're not hungry yet, but by the time …"

"Mom," John interrupted. "Can you believe that …"

Something in his voice got her worried. "What?"

John waited for a long minute and finally "Can you believe that we had a prostitute in our age group?"

"What?" She was so flabbergasted she did not know what else to say.

"A prostitute, Mom," John said pointedly. "She took boys to the ravine."

Sophie, to cover up her real worries, asked, "Did she kiss them?"

Their eyes met. In John's there was horror. "No," he shouted. "It didn't come to that!"

Twilight

ydia was the kind of girl whose curves and curly blond hair down to her waist would stop traffic and could cause an accident on the road. She knew it and was happy. Her life was perfect. The school where she worked had given her a room in a communal apartment. She had a job that she loved as a geography teacher. And of course there was Denis, a math teacher whom she met in the school and fell in love with. Moscow was beautiful at this time of year. Spring smelled of lilacs and hopes and possibilities.

Denis and Lydia had been together for three months, and the relationship was going well. Right now on her narrow bed they were glued to each other, naked. Lydia, her eyes half shut with pleasure, said, "It was so good."

Denis embraced her even more tightly and said, "Let's get married." Lydia nodded her head. She was drowning in joy and disbelief. Denis said, "Let's get married and get out of here."

Lydia laughed. "Where would we go?" She looked around. "Don't you like it here?" Her first-floor room was small but sunny. She had decorated it with flowers in a ceramic vase, a bright synthetic rug that her parents had given her as a housewarming gift, a framed photograph of Lenin, proudly hanging above her desk.

Stroking her incredibly soft and golden hair, Denis said, "To Israel."

Lydia froze for a moment, then slightly moved away from him. She opened her eyes wide as if waking up from a nightmare. "Where?" Denis started covering her with kisses, but Lydia resisted. "What did you say?"

It was around 5 p.m., and the sun was going down rapidly, making room for the upcoming moon. The sound of a tram outside the open window and church bells broke into the room like invaders. Denis said, "Lydia, wake up. It's 1975. Everyone is leaving. It is insane to stay in this country. The system suffocates people."

Lydia, who appeared to fall mute for a moment, seemingly inhaled deeply to get back her speech. She said, "But only the Jews are leaving, so far as I know. Normal people don't run like rats. They stay here in the country that raised them, educated them, loved them." Lydia covered up her nakedness with the blanket.

Denis grabbed cigarettes and matches from the night table. "Loved them?!" He burst out coughing. And having finished, said calmly, "I understand you don't remember 1937 and what followed. You're too young. We both are. But you're an educated woman who has eyes and ears, and who can think and read. What, you don't know about Stalin's atrocities? About people disappearing? People shot, sent to the Gulag, tormented in the cellars of the Lyubyanka? This information didn't find its way into your heart and brain? Everybody suffered, but Jews suffered the most and still do. Did you hear about Stalin's orders to move all the Jews to Birobidzhan, and how the train cars were ready to take them? Thank God Stalin died before it happened. "

Lydia became breathless with indignation. "You too? Against Stalin? Maybe you're against Lenin as well?"

"Both of them were criminals and sent people to death—for political reasons. You're saying this country raised us, educated us, loved us? You're an idiot if you don't understand what went on and is still going on. And Jews are running for their lives." It became darker in the room, with the only light coming from the streetlamp by which Denis could see Lydia's upset and righteous face. He screamed, "My mother is a Jew, did you know that? And in Jewish tradition, if your mother is a Jew, you are a Jew. So there—I am a Jew. Am I a rat?"

At first Lydia wanted to offer a flood of explanations, but they gathered and imploded like an unexpected tsunami, washing words away from her, leaving her mouth swaddled in seaweed, wrapping into a stupor. After a long silence, she murmured breathlessly, "Please. I really want you to go."

Denis, trying to soften his tone, came closer to her and said, "We will figure it out."

But she retreated to the corner of the bed, holding herself in her own arms and said, "Go away. Goodnight."

Headlights from the passing cars peered into the room. Denis went to the front door. His fingers grew clumsy, the flimsy lock opened, and he walked out.

Behind, in the room suffused with cigarette smoke, her bones aching as if she had been beaten or had a fever, Lydia noticed how a layer of dust the color of ash was starting to cover everything in the room. She got up and pulled the blinds down. Her mind went blank. The room submerged into absolute darkness.

The Schnitzel Night

This was their night—the "Schnitzel Night," the two couples called it. Two schnitzels were offered for the price of one on Tuesdays. Their hearts and palates desired the schnitzel so much that they skipped over Fridays as if they did not exist, became progressively angry with each other on Saturdays, and tried to forget Sundays altogether. On Mondays they were so impatient that each couple had to make love using the act as some sort of meditation. When Tuesday arrived, the four of them had to wait a little longer until 7 p.m., when they would meet facing each other at their regular places at the table outside the restaurant. Finally there, they were alert and tranquil at the same time, as if waiting for a train.

"Where are the roses?" asked Armand, approaching the table with big hurrying steps after having parked his car.

"I couldn't help it," said Uma, bursting into laughter but suddenly stopping in the middle of it as if paralyzed. "Darling, I gave them to a homeless man. I wanted him to share my joy."

Mina rebelled. "Oh, Armand, please sit down. Are we ordering a big pretzel to start with? We usually share one."

But Armand kept his mind on the roses. "They were so beautiful. Long-stemmed …"

"They were mine," Uma insisted. "You brought them for me, after all. I had the right to do with them whatever I wanted. I agree they were lovely. But now that I have given them away, they will never die but will live in my memory, will reach eternity."

Mina said to the waitress, "As usual, one pretzel and four schnitzels." Turning to her husband Roy, who was sitting calmly next to her, she asked, "What are we drinking?"

Roy and Armand said in a single voice, "Beer. Wine."

"Two beers, two house wines," Mina raised her hand. "Please, let us be in peace at least on schnitzel night, so everyone behave!"

"But why didn't you keep the roses, Uma?" Armand was getting angry.

With enormous timidity, Roy announced, "It's my birthday today."

Mina exclaimed, "Dear, of course. That's so lovely."

The beer and wine were brought and placed on the table. "Let's celebrate," said Uma in the direction of Roy with a glass in her outstretched hand. "Happy birthday, Roy."

Everyone drank. "You see," said Armand bitterly, "those roses would have been so appropriate on the table. They would have made the atmosphere more festive. And now there's nothing to look at except this stupid pretzel and mustard."

"Just this once, can you *not* complain?" said Uma. "Look at me and feel festive. There's a whole bouquet of me. Don't you agree, Roy?"

"You're a rose yourself," said Mina—who was devastatingly good-looking and slightly shivering in her cashmere shawl.

Armand ordered another beer and finished it surprisingly fast, even before the schnitzels were served. He slammed his empty mug on the table, and sounding a bit drunk, said to Uma, "I want a divorce!"

"What?!" Mina muttered not looking at anyone in particular.

Uma was calm and smiling. "I knew to give the roses away, but you know what, Armand? I haven't heard anything more perfect in my life than what you just said."

Roy's mouth opened in disbelief. "What color were the roses?" was the only thing he could ask.

"Just out of curiosity," Uma's voice became a bit agitated, "What is the reason? Why now, may I ask?"

Armand glanced at Mina, who was intensely involved in examining her bright red fingernails. He closed his eyes. "Because I want to start anew. To try walking different roads before it's too late, to experience the sun, the moon …Maybe become a cosmonaut…"

"With your fear of heights? Of course." Uma kept on smiling.

Armand's face contorted and a few tears rolled down from under his closed eyes.

Hot, steamy schnitzel finally appeared on the table. For some reason, it made them uncomfortable. They looked away from each other. Holding onto their private thoughts, they did not notice how the light had dimmed into darkness and the signs of elusive hopes had invaded their bodies. They finally peered around with their nearsighted eyes. Nothing had changed.

But then they saw the roses. A large unkept hand had put them in the middle of the table, where they looked like a flooding blood stain. The homeless man, his back to the table, was leaving in an unknown direction. His jolty gait suggested he felt free and happy.

This particular Tuesday evening was coming to a close. The empty plates were taken away. No one had a desire for dessert except Uma, who ordered strawberry crepes with whipped cream on top.

"The schnitzel was exceptionally tasty today. I really enjoyed it," said Roy. "How about coffee, everyone?"

Waiting for the coffee, everyone started talking about aliens and how it was rumored that aliens had sex in secret tunnels.

When total darkness invaded the sky, they asked for a candle. Roy said that in the total darkness he had seen the symbol of the cross.

"Oh, yes?" said Mina. "And what do you see now in this flickering candlelight my darling?"

"You are too presumptuous, dear wife, if you think I can see anything without being confused."

"Oh, how interesting. Do proceed, Roy," said Uma, visibly amused.

Armand interrupted. "A good story needs wine or beer or any kind of liquor."

They waited, but the waitress did not come back for a long time, and the conversation fell flat.

"Okay," said Uma finally. "Bad as it may be, there's always next Tuesday."

Lucky in Love

$\mathcal{I}$ think that only recently I began to understand the preciousness of life. I became calmer. I discovered that both "Hell" and "Paradise" existed on earth. One only had to choose where one wanted to be.

This is what happened some time ago. My mother asked me to meet her for lunch. She suggested this lovely vegetarian café she knew I liked near Aventura Mall in North Miami. I was a bit surprised because she was a "meat-and-pasta" kind of person. I walked in and immediately saw her sitting at a window table, a big smile on her youngish blue-eyed face.

"Over here," she motioned me with her hand adorned with rings my late father had been showering her with. She was not alone. A man of about my age (I am fifty-five) sat next to her eyeing me.

He got up when I approached and extended his hand. "Kenneth," he said, "very nice to meet you.

"Likewise. Sophia, but you already knew that." I smiled thinking, *Oh hell! Matchmaking? Mama, how many times have I told you? I'm happy the way things are. Leave me alone. But no! Here you go again …*

"Sit down, sit down, Sophie darling. Kenneth wanted to meet you so much. I hope you don't mind. Besides, it's time the two of you got to know each other. Here is a menu, dear. Look at it. What would you like? We already know what we want. The waiter said salads here are very good with quinoa and avocado – the healthy things you like."

My mother was a woman who had been leaving everything unsaid—my father's illness that took him to his grave, her winning some kind of award —not a Pulitzer Prize, but an award nonetheless—for a fur coat design she had made. The Italian fashion house Fendi had loved it and afterwards they commissioned all their fur designs from her. She also never commented on when I divorced my husband or about my haircuts, my losing or gaining weight. But recently she had become unusually talkative. "You're 55 now, not getting any younger. Time to put your personal life in order. You need someone by your side. Sweetheart, it's time to begin dating." I had told her to *please just stop* but she would not retreat to her reclusive silence.

After we ordered food—avocado toast for me, vegetarian hamburger for Ken (though I was sure he would prefer a real one), and steamed veggies for my mother (who coquettishly claimed she was watching her figure)—Ken addressed me. "So, your mom says you are a writer. How interesting. Would I have read anything you have written?" He smiled and took a drink of his water.

"Do you have children?" I asked, diagnosing him at the same time—pleasant, good-looking, humor in his eyes.

He spread his arms. "Sorry, no, unfortunately. I don't."

"Well then, I write books for kids. You definitely have not read them."

He turned to my mother and shrugged. "Such is life."

"Well," said my mother, "maybe one day ..." They both smiled, as if they knew something I didn't.

Aha, I thought, *they are in cahoots. Damn it! I know what my mother wants, but him? Young for a man, fit, head full of hair, he could do much better than me.*

Our orders came and we started eating. From time to time each of us made comments about the food (delicious, yummy, salubrious!), the weather (warm, sunny), and a Spanish telenovela that Mom and I watched while Ken looked puzzled. Ken glanced outside and said something about a photo-session and the light being perfect for it. "I apologize, but I need to go. The light is a fleeting tool I have to run after."

"No coffee?" my mother said with disappointment.

"No. Thank you, darling, I really have to go. It was great meeting you, Sophie. I hope to see you again soon. Good luck with your children's stories."

"Good luck with the light," I said politely. He left.

"So?" My mother's eyes shone with excitement. "What did you think? Did you like him? Isn't he a darling? He's an artist, a photographer."

Of course, I thought, but aloud I said, "Whom does he photograph? Naked whores?" I was already stupidly jealous of all those young, gorgeous girls he was probably undressing through his camera.

"No! No!" said my mother almost violently. "Nothing like that. He is a poet of nature. You should see his work. It's so unusual, as if he imprisons beauty, creates a timeless memory of it, and gives you a chance to recognize it. He is a magician."

"Oh, Mama!" I laughed. "You talk as if you are in love with him. I mean, he is pleasant and all, not bad looking. I just really don't …"

"But I am in love with him! Oh my God. Here, I've actually said it aloud. I am in love with Ken! And he is in love with me." My mother closed her eyes and covered her cheeks. She was blushing. It seemed to be a happy blush.

I looked at her in disbelief. "But Mama, how old is he?"

"Fifty-eight."

"And you? Do you know how old you are?"

"Yes, I do. None of that matters. We love each other."

I did not know whether to laugh or cry.

"He gives me everything—freedom and intimacy. Tons of affection, no demands. He doesn't care how old I am.

"Mom!" I thought for a minute. "Do you give him money?" She didn't answer. "It's risky," I said. "Do you understand? It's very risky."

"Well," my mother looked a bit less enthusiastic but still hopeful, "I do, and I don't."

"What do you mean, Ma?"

"I don't just *give* him money. I give him money to invest."

"You what?" I let out a long and bitter whistle. "How much money did you give him to invest?"

"Well, all of it."

"How much?"

"Listen, Sophie. I don't understand anything in finances."

"I know. That's why you have an accountant and a financial adviser."

"But Ken is better than all of them. He took my $300,000 and turned it into a million."

"How do you know he turned it into a million?"

"He told me so. It actually is all much better than it sounds." My mother's eyes were pleading with me.

"It sounds like a bad joke," I said. "But we all fall for the wrong man at some point in our lives." I was thinking of my ex-husband. The sun was coming down.

The next day I sent my accountant to check on my mother's financial affairs. He said that everything was in order and that, indeed, she had a million dollars to her name. "There was some unexpected merger of two companies, and the stock skyrocketed," the accountant said. "Your mom became a millionaire."

So, I thought, Ken wasn't a "wrong man." And even when his physical self moved on to another romantic object, he left my mother with a million dollars. But then Mom had always been lucky in love.

Friends

It was Sunday afternoon. I didn't want to do anything, so I called my friend Sally and asked if she wanted to do nothing with me. The two of us met at a coffee shop, but neither wanted coffee or food. We ordered two glasses of white wine. Chardonnay.

"So," I said, "how's it going?"

She smacked her lips after a long, big gulp of Chardonnay. "Fine. You?"

"Fine," I said, knowing that nothing was fine. No job—fired. No money—spent. No children—just didn't happen. No husband —he had recently left me for someone else. We looked at each other. "Wanna see a movie?" I asked.

She shook her head and emptied her glass.

"Another one?"

"No," she said. "I better be going …"

She got up. "That was short," I said. "Okay then. See you soon."

She quickly was on her way to the door, then turned her head, looked at me and came back. Next, I felt her beautiful mouth on my ear, "Feeling sorry for yourself? You're not good enough for him." She straightened, blew me a kiss, and left. This time for good, it seemed.

Her perfume lingered in the air. "Okay, Baby," I whispered to myself. "Just wonder, how long will it take for you to hear those exact same words from his next conquest, bitch?" I was deep in thought for a while and then went back to my Chardonnay.

The Sound of Bells

The sound of church bells always grounded Maria in the reality of the day. She would stop whatever she was doing at the moment and go into her internal self. She would stay there without thinking, only feeling a joy that seized her. And covered by it, she would retreat into its gentle waves. Afterwards, she knew exactly what she wanted in life—nothing more than what she already had. She would be forgiven. She would incarnate into someone else—dangerous, attractive, going easily through the experience of living, utterly moral, sometimes immoral, fragile, never harming others, or so she hoped. The bells would trail off, and she would stop and resume her life. Not an honest life. Shameful, really.

A wife and a mother by night and morning, a call girl by the afternoon under a false name, Eve, she did not allow herself to think about her secret life that she could slip into so easily while tending to her domestic duties. But in the silence of the empty house, she needed to talk openly about that other life that had *not* been forced on her. She had chosen it because it held some unidentifiable attraction that she was unable to resist.

Her favorite time of the day was when the morning avalanche had been taken care of—kids safely at school, husband at work, dishes washed and put away—and she, finally in total isolation could transform inwardly and outwardly into a fictional character of her own invention. She delighted in being able to act out all the crazy ideas that her imagination provided.

Smiling severely in front of the mirror, she would attempt a dark brown lipstick to emphasize the cruel streak of mind of her imagined personage. She did not need the permission of her husband to dress or make herself up according to her own tastes. Yes! Maria had a husband, and she was *not* cheating on him, all the time thinking how her escapades were her own and belonged only to her. The mysterious energy that she experienced in her body at those moments fed her mind.

"Great," she thought, "I gave myself permission to write a book that no one will ever read. And that's the whole point. I won't be abused, admired, hated by anyone. And I don't need a pencil and a pad."

She laughed, remembering how it all had started when a nice-looking middle-aged woman sat next to her in the park, whose delightful personality Maria could not resist. The woman, Clementina, was funny and bold and talked about a million things, all of which were new to Maria. She felt an immediate connection. "Bells in Bethesda?" Clementina laughed. "You, honey, are hallucinating or else have a great imagination. Come and visit me sometime. How about tomorrow? Coffee at 12?" Clementina got up. "I have to go, beautiful. Here is my card." Attorney-at-law the card said.

When Maria arrived at a Victorian house painted white and rang the bell, the door was opened immediately. Clementina, talking nonstop, ushered her into a small but cozy sitting room. "You don't look as if you have a sixteen-year-old child, dear."

Maria nodded. "Yes, and a twelve-year-old."

"Well, twelve I could see." Wearing a multicolored kaftan dress, Clementina was pouring red wine into Maria's glass.

"Oh no, I already had one. It's enough for me."

The doorbell rang, and accompanied by Clementina's secretary-receptionist, a fit, tan, gray-haired gentleman came in smiling broadly. "Clementina darling, I was in the neighborhood and decided to pay you an unscheduled visit." The gentleman and Clementina kissed hello.

"Oh, Sandro. You don't need an appointment with me. You are always welcome." Clementina introduced Maria to Sandro as Eve, a woman "who recently has rediscovered herself." Maria was finishing her second glass of chianti when Sandro offered that she taste a fantastically expensive whiskey that he had brought with him.

"So, Eve, tell me. What are the astonishing discoveries you've made about your gorgeous self? I'm all ears."

The two of them were sitting on a loveseat, and Sandro's face was so close to Maria's that she could feel his ear rubbing across her cheek. Clementina dissipated like a cloud. And making no effort to resist, Maria collapsed into Sandro's arms.

This had been her first stint among the many that followed during her two-year gig at the "attorney-at-law's place" that put fire into her everyday existence. She considered herself an actress and a writer. And maybe it was a far stretch, but she did not think so, as she became more and more skillful in creating her characters and performing them.

She organized her time wisely, and no one at home noticed her changes. There she was "Mama" or "Ma" or "Mother" or "Maria." Her escalation in the art of deceit brought her more money than she had ever dreamed of. Oh yes, she was paid handsomely. She was admiring herself for writing a great book that no one would ever read, a book of wonders. A book that opened windows and doors she never had known existed. "It's a gift," she told herself. Her "Eve" had many identities, even though most of the people she worked with were silent and did not ask a lot of questions. They were discreet about themselves and not too curious about her. Sometimes someone would ask where she was from. Because of her accent, she supposed. The answer depended on whom she wanted to be at that particular moment—a gymnast from Ukraine, a singer from Georgia, a mathematician from Sweden, a nurse from France, a dancer, a pilot, a devout Christian, a Jew …Her place of birth was always exotic, as were the outfits Clementina kept for her in one of her closets.

The place had its own regulations: A strict time for the appointments—for her it was 12 noon or two p.m. while her kids were at school. No checks, only cash—and only through Clementina. The length of time—no more than an hour and a half. The rooms could be partially lighted or totally dark. There was a special menu for an additional price. All arrangements were to be discussed with

Clementina.

It never even occurred to Maria to suggest any dishes from the "special menu" to her husband. She felt like a psychologist who had sworn to keep her trade separate from the rest of her life. "Theater," she sometimes thought to herself. "Pure theater." And she loved it.

One afternoon Clementina met her excitedly. "Listen, Eve, today is your lucky day. Your client is very good-looking, charming, hungry for new experiences. I told him I would give him our very best. Show him a good time." She laughed. "You lucky dog, Eve. I hope you'll enjoy yourself. I know I would. Oh, by the way, he requested total darkness, probably he's a politician."

To Maria's astonishment, she was a little nervous as she made her way into the darkness of the room. A curious man expecting a miracle—was she up to the challenge? After all, she was almost thirty-nine. Would he like her? Would she be able to fulfill his expectations? How would she greet him? In bed? By the door? Behind a heavy curtain? For the first time she felt some danger in the air. Why? What was different this time? The outfit she chose was simply a black lacy bra and matching panties— almost conservative, she thought. She sat down on the chair and waited.

The room was dark. Only the outline of the furniture was barely visible. A few moments passed, and Maria could not stop shivering. She decided to have some wine. She got up and pushed aside a curtain to see where the bottle and glasses were placed, poured herself a full glass, returned to the chair and drank it all. She closed her eyes.

When she opened them, a bit confused, she realized that she had been dozing and that some time had passed. She looked at her watch. It was 12:15. There was no one else in the room. Suddenly she became aware that she could see things clearly. She looked around and realized she had forgotten to pull the curtain back. She got up and went to the window. When she looked out, she saw the very familiar figure of her son moving away from the house.

Just then she was crushed by the sound of the bells thundering in her ears.

Glass and Fire

The end of September, the perfect time for exhibition openings. People were back in New York from their summer vacations. It seemed that the city was awakening after a deep summer sleep and would have liked to spill out all the secrets that had been suffocating it. Among many exciting happenings Friday night – concerts, plays, operas - Tribeca Gallery opened its doors for the fashionable crowd to pile in at exactly 7 p.m. in anticipation of art, drinks, to see and be seen, discussions of the latest news in the arts and otherwise, and in general to have a good time. A new upcoming glass artist, Vita K.was presenting her work - unusually shaped, glistening glass pieces. One could hear exclamations such as *So young, so talented! Splendid!*

Vita was standing with a glass of red wine in her hands greeting the arrivals. One elderly gentleman came up to her, "Quite unusual to be drinking red wine in a gallery." He chuckled. "But then again it matches the extraordinary exclusiveness of your work. You are the artist, right? Who is your influence?"

Vita smiled. "Why, Dale Chihuly, of course."

"Of course," the gentleman said. "I should have known. You follow his flamboyancy. Your flower arrangements are stunning, luminous, sparkling like miniature suns."

"Thank you. I'm passionate about glass and all shades of red." Vita was about to say something more, but suddenly she noticed a tall blonde woman wading through the crowd. Vita's smile vanished. Four years! She had not seen her for four years! She had almost managed to forget about her – them really – to not think about their indecency, betrayal, vulgarity. Zora was still striking. The blue-grey saucers of her eyes were searching around, jumping up and down, looking for someone. "Zora!" Vita called out despite herself.

The red of Zora's lips stretched into the biggest smile ever seen. In a moment she was already squeezing Vita's small frame, saying "You! You! I found you! I've missed you so much. Look at you, so pretty, so classy. Your own exhibition. You're a star. You've always been the best."

"What about you? Why are you here?" Vita tried to disengage from Zora's strong embrace.

"Me?" Zora lowered her eyes and whispered, "Later. I will tell you everything later."

Vita knew Zora was an experienced liar, so she wasn't in any rush to hear Zora's confessions. "Are you alone?" she asked, scared to hear the answer. She did not want to see Vlad, the man who had broken her world, who even now, four years later, made her heart skip a beat just from the memory of his name.

"I'm alone," Zora said. "Is there any empty corner where we could talk?"

"I only have a minute," Vita did not look into Zora's eyes as if she, Vita, had committed a crime.

"It'll be enough. You know I'm a fast talker." Zora grinned.

Vita led the way to her office separated from the rest of the gallery by glass and closed the door. "So," she said sitting down and indicating a chair for Zora.

"No, I don't have time to sit around. I just wanted to tell you that your Vlad is a scumbag and a piece of shit. He used me for a while and then sold me to a wealthy Saudi Arabian guy named Nahim who took me to his harem in Riyadh where I landed with God knows how many other wives and almost died from boredom being locked in, drowning in a sea of wine and sweets – fucking sweets that I am not able to look at since - under constant surveillance of shaven-headed gorillas. One of the gorillas, faintly reminiscent of a human being, a cousin of Nahim, took pity on me after I offered him my diamond Rolex that Nahim had given me as a wedding present, and helped me to escape." Zora articulated very clearly and to the point. She was still standing by the door, several rows of amber around her neck and on her wrists shining like Vita's glass creations. Vita kept her lips sealed. "I did you a favor," Zora went on, "by seducing that schmuck, your Vlad, and taking him away from you. You were so blinded by his fucking charm, his lies, you didn't see that he was only after your parents' money. I have always wanted to tell that to you, to explain," Zora cast her eyes to the floor, "and to apologize. You needed to know the truth. Now I have to run."

"Sounds a bit familiar, like a book I read by a wife of one of the Bin Laden brothers." Vita rolled her eyes. "Where are you running to?"

"Okay, think what you like, but if you must know, I'm not running to – I'm running from. My Saudi husband, who is a devil and a psychopath, is here in New York looking for me. His cousin gave him the information of my whereabouts under duress, of course, then took pity on me once again and told me about it. So that's the story in brief. I'm glad I found you." Zora took a step towards Vita, extended her hand, and said, "Let's be friends again."

Vita did not move. Zora shrugged her shoulders, "We shall meet again." She flashed a movie star smile, pirouetted, and quickly walked out of Vita's office.

Vita continued to sit there thinking how much she would like to be home now, to lie down on her comfortable sofa with her beloved German shepherd Nika by her side, their hearts beating in unison. She felt a bit feverish. *What if the old man asking me questions was Chihuly himself? Damn! I don't remember if he was wearing an eye-patch. I wonder if he is still there.* Vita got up to go back to the exhibition. She heard a shot. Splashes of blood covered the window and door of her office. Was she losing her mind? One thing was clearly true, where Zora had towered a second ago, she was no more.

Family

There stood Alberto leaning against her porch railing with a smile. "Wow," Cara said, coming out of the front door dressed for jogging. "That's a surprise. When did you arrive?"

"Just now." He turned his head with long black hair away from her towards the burning sun. "It's still early but already so hot. I don't understand how you survive here."

"Yeah, hot, all year round. Unlike where you are now. Where are you actually? Seattle? Oregon? Wyoming?"

"Montana. I love it there," he spat.

"Good," she said. "It's good that you're so far away, and I don't have to see you. You raped me, remember?" Her eyes fogged with unwanted memories.

"I didn't rape you." He dug in his jeans pocket and brought out a pack of Camels. You seduced me."

"What?!"

"You seduced me with your smiles and tricks and Britney impersonations. You came onto me."

"I was rehearsing, you idiot."

"For your burlesque-porno show?" He chuckled, wiping the sweat from his forehead. "Got a light?"

"You know what, get lost." She started down the steps. "I have things to do."

"Wait," he touched her shoulder.

"Don't touch me!"

"It's good to see you."

She hesitated. "You too. Are you still fighting fires?" She blew off a string of hair on her face.

"Yeah."

"Is it dangerous?"

"Sometimes. Got a light?"

She looked straight at him. "I don't smoke anymore." Tears flooded her eyes. She wiped them with her fist. "Let's go to the café. Mom and dad probably already opened it. No matter what, their coffee's good, and dad bakes fine scones."

"That he does."

They started on a dusty road still wet from the night rainfall. "You need flipflops here or sneakers."

"How is dad?" Alberto asked, looking down at his feet dressed in construction boots.

"Dad's dad. Working. Talking. Fighting with mom on every subject. He is a stern democrat, and she is exactly opposite."

Alberto smiled. "And how is mom?"

"Not aging. Pretty as ever." Cara smiled too.

"You take after her. You know what I mean. Pretty."

"Well," Cara said quietly, lifting her nose into the hot air, "you look like dad, tall and all." They kept silent for a moment, then she sighed. "Imagine, if they had never met and married, your dad wouldn't have adopted me, and my mom would not have adopted you. We would have been strangers. We could have bumped into each other in the universe and lived happily ever after."

"Stranger things have happened," Alberto grunted.

"Yes, like me doing my own laundry," Cara laughed.

"I didn't rape you."

"I know."

The morning kept deciding whether to stream more sunrays or sprinkle the earth with water. But it did not bother them as they walked and listened to the sounds of nature awakening around them.

Going Forward

Sun shining through the glass into my eyes, waking me up. The morning has started as all the other mornings lately. The happy thought of fresh brewed coffee that I will have to make myself; the exercise class at 9:45 that I religiously attend in the hope to lose weight; then my work for some non-profit that pays my bills. I don't even have to leave my studio apartment, the one I could not afford after my husband left for a much younger, prettier, skinnier me. He told me so himself, "She looks exactly like you twenty years ago." I am thirty-eight, so she must be eighteen, I figure. Good for him. I understand and am not at all mad at him. I'm mad at myself when I look in the mirror. How could it have happened? But it didn't just happen. I am the sole reason for it.

Take this tee-shirt I am wearing. Ben, my husband, got it for me ten years ago in Mexico City's famous *Lucha libre* wrestling ring. Life was fun then. We loved each other, or we thought we did. Ben left, but the tee-shirt stayed. I wear it almost every day to the gym. It has lost its shape, colors, fabric thickness, has holes all over from multiple washings, but it's still my favorite. It gives me the trust and stability that one usually gets from a dog. I don't have a dog. I have my old, ripped, shapeless tee-shirt. I'm pathetic. That's it.

Last night I had a dream that I was giving a party to which six people came, each wearing an African face mask of different colors —red for life, gold for fortune, blue for innocence, green for earth, white for mother's milk. I read about the meaning of the colors of the masks on the internet after I woke up. I instinctively knew—the way you *"just know"* in dreams—that behind those masks were women related to me, all of them now dead. The red mask was my grandmother, whom I loved intensely. The gold was my great-grandmother, who single-handedly supported herself and her thirteen children after her husband's death. Blue—my mother's twin sister, my best friend whom I followed like a puppy. Green —my mother's older sister, who, as the legend goes, saved her family from starvation during World War II due to her beauty. She was working at a factory, and a high official fell in love with her and was secretly giving her extra food ration coupons. White was my mother, of course, who recently passed away, and I miss her every day.

In the dream, my mother whispered in my ear, "Your aunt is completely clear of cancer. You can call her now and hang out with her as you did before." I was happy and scared at the same time. In reality at the age of forty-six, she died of cancer. Her husband divorced her after he found out that her breasts were going to be removed. It turned out he didn't actually have to—she expired six months later.

My great-grandmother died on Rosh Hashana. She prepared a kosher chicken that she managed to obtain in impoverished Moscow, got tired standing on her feet (no one knew precisely her age), lay down to stretch her limbs, and never got up again.

My grandmother was basically killed in a hospital through ignorance and negligence. And maybe, but just maybe, by her own desire to finally rest. Her husband had died in the beginning of the war, so she was left alone with her three girls—three sisters, as in the famous play. It was tough for an uneducated woman with no skills but an obligation to survive.

Then, still in the dream, Ben showed up and asked me why I had invited him. I said I had just wanted to see him, nothing more. And now that I had seen him, he could leave. "Still wearing the tee-shirt?" he smirked.

The sun is up and burning. I should start moving, or I'll be late for my class. Not to forget this big plastic bag with Ben's clothes that he has still not removed, as if I have so much space in this tiny apartment. Miami has become very expensive lately, but I love it here. Unlike cold and gray Moscow, it's sunny all the time. Fascinating! The idea comes to me to give Ben's clothes to Justin, my gym instructor, who is approximately the same size as Ben and who has been wearing the same clothes for all the six months I have known him. Obviously, he is a poor young fellow, so why not help? I feel charitable and good. The bag is heavy. I hope Justin will like Ben's idea of "cool."

After the class ends, I wait until everyone has left and go up to Justin, who is sweaty in a sexy kind of way. I tell him it has been a great class and I have enjoyed it, ask where he learned how to do it, and whether this was what he intends to do the rest of his life, (thinking how he could survive on $17 an hour teaching one or two hours a day.) He must be very poor. Does he have any money to eat, to pay rent? I really want to help.

Justin smiles at me. "What's your name again?" he asks.

I say, "Maria."

"Maria, what a beautiful name. Where are you from? I hear your accent."

"From Russia."

"Oh, an immigrant." His face shows sympathy. "I understand. It's tough." And he stares at my dilapidated tee-shirt.

"And you?" I asked.

"I'm from here, Miami."

"Are you enjoying teaching aerobics?" I try not to sound condescending.

He laughs. "Am I teaching? I just exercise, and others follow me, which is great. The exercises bring oxygen to my brain and make it work harder. I need it, because I'm working on a certain A-I problem that could become crucial for companies. I used to work for Amazon, made tons of money, so that now I don't have to stress over doing what I really like—to develop my own idea into reality."

Oh my God, I think, what am I going to do with this stupid plastic bag filled with Ben's old clothes?

Justin says, "I have another class now." He hesitates. "Would you like to have a cup of coffee with me afterwards?"

On the way to the ladies' lounge, I notice a counter where among some health food, cell phone chargers, drinks, they sell tee-shirts with the club's logo. I buy one. Then I proceed to the showers, marveling at the idea of throwing my *Lucha libre* tee-shirt and the plastic bag into the garbage. I suddenly feel free. Maybe my dream was telling me what to do with my freedom, perhaps to travel to Africa.

Later that afternoon when I return home after a lovely coffee vacation with Justin, searching for evidence of an initial spark between us and hoping it was there, I receive a text from Ben. "I'm planning on stopping by tomorrow to pick up my stuff." I laugh hysterically. Good luck, honey. Good luck.

The Act of Love

*A*fter all, thought Letitia, *what is the act of love? Is it sharing a sandwich? Helping someone who is in need? Coming to a rescue? Cooking a meal? Having a glass of wine together? Shedding a tear for five hundred Americans stuck in Kabul and millions of Afghan women who might be subjected to slavery or killed?*

She fiddled with this question for a while, then decided it was time to go downstairs to order pizza—and eat it with the man of her dreams who was still asleep in her bedroom. She was a florist. Of course, she had wanted to be an actress but supported herself by being a florist. She set up a shop on money she had made working as a reader for the disabled. She made flower arrangements using branches, leaves, metal sticks, wood, wicker baskets, and other things. One of the arrangements was called "Stairway to the Sky," which she entered in a local competition and won, receiving the title of "Fabulous Florist" and $1,000. That brought her more work than she could manage, so she looked for help.

Adam had shown up in her shop eager to work. His main talent was to make people happy. He made her happy. She had to hire one additional employee who would actually do the work, a young girl named Clarissa, with tattoos and nose rings. For Adam work was play. After Letitia would finish with her flowery creations, he would add a chunk of watermelon, half an avocado, an oversized tomato ready to burst, pears so ripe that juice oozed out of them. He would call those arrangements the process of life and death. Letitia thought of them as very imaginative. She was falling in love.

Letitia picked up her order and ran up the stairs so that the pizza wouldn't get cold, since she knew Adam hated cold pizza. As she entered the apartment, Adam had already made the bed and was sitting in the kitchen with a coffee mug in his hand watching TV. "Oh, my God, the Taliban is going to destroy that country," Letitia said. "It's so awful."

"What's up?" Adam said.

"Here. Food for you."

"Thank you. You're a gem."

"Please turn the TV off," Letitia said. "I can't take it anymore. It's so sad. I have a question I want to ask you."

"Oh, so do I. Who goes first?" He looked excited, like a child anticipating a nod from his parents for good behavior.

"You do," Letitia said.

"Okay. So, I've been thinking. When is the competition? Tomorrow, isn't it? What if we double our chances of winning the first prize? "

"What do you mean?"

"What I mean is that you and I go solo as separate entities, so if you win, it's our win, and if I win, it's our win. So instead of one shot, we'll have two, like a double espresso." He smiled. "Come here. You're the best espresso I've ever had. I love to cover your espresso with my milk foam. Together we're a cappuccino."

"You're a poet," Letitia said. "In reality, I'm a black girl in love with a white guy. So what?"

"So, nothing. We'll win the money. We'll enlarge the shop. And we'll live happily ever after." Adam managed to make it sound nice and easy and not threatening at all. Their romance seemed strong and endless.

She was done with acting. "Fine," Letitia said. "Now it's my turn."

"Okay."

"What do you think an act of love is?"

Adam's creation called "Gateway to Hell" was monumental. It mesmerized and crushed and lifted all at the same time. Hell was not scary anymore. It was only a continuation of life. Letitia's was a sweet simple act of a person who did not really have a concept. Roses, peonies, orchids, carnations in a thick cluster were appealing but had no ecstasy. No one would climb over a cliff for it. She called it "Flames," but she herself understood there were no flames, only aesthetic concerns.

Letitia won. After all the necessary congratulatory banalities ended, she looked for Adam but could not find him. He disappeared. His phone was turned off. She suddenly realized that she knew Adam only within two vicinities, her apartment, and the shop. He had vaguely mentioned living somewhere in Bushwick in an apartment with two or three other roommates. That was all she knew. She had waited for him with a bottle of celebratory champagne late into the night. Her curtains were glowing with the suggestion of moonlight passing by. He never showed up or called. *Perhaps it's just as well*, she thought, *I might have been pulled into slavery like those poor Afghan women.*

Next morning, she went to the shop a bit late, hoping that Adam would already be there. She had given him the keys some time ago. She felt overdosed on champagne from the night before, and a hangover clouded her vision. The shop was empty. But Adam's absence had not settled in the store yet. His empty pack of Marlboros was on one of the counters, his damp extra-large gardening gloves next to it. His "Hell" was installed on the front counter towering over everything, including her thoughts. The "Hell" was magnificent.

Clarissa, the young employee, ran through the door breathless. "I am so sorry I'm late."

Still looking at the "Hell," Letitia asked Clarissa, "Hey, what do you think is an act of love?"

"Screwing," said Clarissa, without missing a beat.

Letitia turned her head to Clarissa's shapely eighteen-year-old body, her curls picked up by a rubber band, and thought to herself, "Right."

"Oh, by the way," Clarissa said, busying herself with sweeping the floor, emptying the garbage can. "Adam stopped by last night. I was still here. Said he won't be coming any more. Got another opportunity somewhere upstate New York or something. Asked me if I want to go with him. I said no, though he is a good fuck." She thought for a second.

"But you must know. Weren't you and him an item? Anyway, I love Brooklyn."

"Too bad, honey," Letitia said.

"Why?"

"'Cause I'm going to close the shop. It takes too much of my time."

"What do you need time for?"

"For auditions. After all, the theater is where I belong." At that moment, she really believed in what she was saying.

In the Park

The park in the afternoon has been washed by a recent rain. An old man leans against his cane that looks more like a gigantic root of a tree. There are many sounds in the air – the barking of a dog, the rustling of grass, a child's cry of joy.

The child catches a butterfly. The butterfly is flapping its wings; it is trembling terribly. The boy's fingers lose their grip. The insect flies to the ground. The boy runs to his mother. He stops short at the sight of an intruder. A woman is sitting next to his mother, and both smile. The woman has an unfamiliar smell. The two speak a foreign language – Russian, his mother's language. They seem very happy. The boy is forgotten by his mother. The dog licks the boy's leather sandals through which his colorful socks show.

"Don't be scared," the woman says. "It's a very friendly dog." The dog barks like mad and wags its tail. The woman pats the dog.

This dog is not the kind of dog the boy would like to have one day.

The dog, a small dachshund, goes away to sniff at the old man's shiny black shoes. He is a gentleman – the old man, that is. He wears a hat. His felt hat is blown onto the lawn. The old man stretches his hand to touch the dog and loses his balance. His cane is now lying on the grass. The grass has different colors – bright and shadowy shades of green, depending on the position of the sun. The sun spreads its rays over the old man's body.

The boy's mother and her new friend, the woman stranger, help the man back onto the bench and into his meditation on the world of the park. And it is at this moment that the woman, slapping her forehead, says to the boy's mother, "Masha, dear, I completely forgot. Can you do me a favor and stay with my dog? It won't take long. I need to run to the laundromat; they've probably thrown my laundry out."

The boy is upset. He does not want his mother to have any new friends.

"The old man is all right," his mother says. "Don't panic, Mark. You are such a worrier, like a rabbi or something. Don't concern yourself with all the problems of the world."

"I have been sent to this earth as a prophet, Mama. You know I'm psychic. I can see things you can't. For instance that stranger woman, she is a sorceress."

"Oh God!" his mother laughs. She kisses the boy and takes his light body into her arms. The old man smiles. There is no other butterfly to be caught. The air is clear; it is September.

"I hate Sundays," the stranger woman offers when she comes back, her neatly folded laundry squeezed under her armpit.

"Do you have a family?" the boy's mother asks.

The woman nods and says, "I have a husband to take care of. My daughter is married and lives separately."

"You look very young to have a married daughter. I don't have a husband. It's just Mark and me." And then they start long monologues in Russian with such speed, half the time the boy does not understand the words they use. He stops trying to follow them and looks at the old man, who is determined to get up without help.

Having succeeded, the old man says, "Thank you again. It was a pleasure to meet all four of you," and he waves the hand that holds his hat. He disappears between the forest of bushes in the direction of the main avenue. The boy is unsure whether his mother or that other creature, the stranger woman, understood what the old man said. The boy is not in the mood to translate. The playground in the shade of an oak tree does not interest him anymore. He would prefer to cross the park to the other side and join the old man. But as they leave the park, he follows the two women. His mother is leading the stranger woman's dog on the leash.

The boy is right, of course. His mother and the stranger woman from the park become such good friends that it sickens him. It is unnatural: they drink tea together, go shopping, talk on the phone, and during those timeless chats his mother disgustingly openly tells the other woman every detail of her private life – about the boy's grades at school, what they will have for dinner, about grandmother's calls from Moscow, and the boy's sore throat, about his mother's loneliness and her difficult life without a man. Without a man?! And who does she think he, her son, is? Is he some kind of animal, or maybe a girl? This is too much. He feels the need to undertake something, the need for immediate action. He gets ill.

The first to come in, before even a doctor, is that dreadful woman with her witch-like long hair. She knows best, she brings the medicine. He is forced to swallow some bitter stuff at daybreak. His head is heavy. The woman is a poisonous pill herself: he wants to spit her out. The woman is insistent; she won't give up. She puts her cold fishy hand on the boy's eyes to make him blind, he guesses. With her hoarse voice she yells a lullaby into his aching chest.

The lullaby is the kind the boy's grandmother used to sing to him when he was a baby. The boy remembers his grandmother's warm hands. This woman is a thief – she is stealing his grandmother's song. He hates the woman for doing that.

But soon he is indifferent and cool and detached and tired. He protests no more. His stoicism is noticed by the wicked woman. She says to the boy's mother, "Look, Masha, he has learned to love me. I am not the type to surrender. See? He holds my hand."

A great day comes! Though the boy's mother does not count the days of the week, this Saturday is special. It is warm outside. The boy wakes up and looks out the window. From the street many faces are glued to his windowpane. The faces are of his friends, boys and girls of the neighborhood. The children are of different ages from about five to thirteen. They are invited to his party at eleven o'clock at McDonald's. It is nine-thirty in the morning now of the day of his birth. His mother tells him the story over and over again how in the hospital the nurse brought her a girl, and she – his mother – immediately recognized the mistake. Her son didn't look like that! He looked like a man from the beginning.

His friends are now dressed up and peer through the window. Their cheeks are washed and shine in the bright sun.

McDonald's is two blocks away. In a vivid caravan the children hurry there. Including the boy's mother, they are eight people. Eight beautiful "Happy Meals" are on the table followed by a cake from Carvel next door. There are eight candles on the white and blue of the ice cream cake – seven plus one for good luck. The boy gives his mother a look of happiness.

At night it is a different matter. Again there is that awful woman and other guests. The boy takes refuge in the walk-in closet, the one feature of their home of which his mother is proud. He goes through the presents he received in the morning from his friends: a box of pencils, paints and a brush; and album for drawing; several stickers with stars and moons.

The stars and the moons become wet from his falling tears. The boy bitterly sobs at the thought that his mother day after day gives him for lunch the most horrible bologna sandwiches. Every time he forgets to tell her how much he hates them. He feels suffocated inside the closet.

The boy almost falls asleep on the comfortable pile of clothes that he has pulled onto the floor from the hangers. He hears the telephone ring. His mother's joyful voice. The boy is excited. It is Moscow. His grandmother or perhaps his favorite uncle Kolya is calling.

His other uncle Sergei lives somewhere nearby in New York in a church with strangers. That church is for Jews, or the Jews are for this church. The boy doesn't exactly understand. But his mother hangs up the phone when Sergei calls. She says he has betrayed the whole Jewish people, and she cries. That woman, her new friend – the boy knows her name starts with the letter L, but he does not care to remember. L. tells his mother not to hang up the phone but to reconcile with Sergei – baptized or not, it does not matter – and to keep him close to her heart. The boy's mother sighs and says she will do it but that she needs time.

The boy runs out of the closet to pick up the phone, but something is wrong with the line. He can hear nothing. L. opens her purse and gives the boy his present. It is beautifully wrapped in two shades of blue – the paper is light like the morning sky, but the bow is dark like the sea at night. The boy tears the paper away without any consideration of its form or shape. Underneath – oh, he cannot believe it. He is shaking inside. He turns his back and takes his treasure with him to the closet. "Thank you," he murmurs on the way.

"The boy needs a father!" He hears L.'s determined voice say.

Music is his lifesaver. He adores all forms it takes – loud, soft, classical, modern, his mother's humming in the kitchen, or a brass band's thunder in the park. L. could not have known, and the boy's mother would never had asked for such an expensive gift, a radio with headphones. L., the witch, obviously found out from one of her voodoo connections. The boy puts the headphones on and tunes the radio to a song he likes. The song is about a man, a musician. He plays the piano and sings. And everybody, including the witch, stands around his piano and hums in unison with his song.

As the boy grows up, he learns by heart the story his mother tells about his seventh birthday and how he fell asleep in the closet.

Life changes with the appearance of a certain dress in their house. The dress is gray, not the dull gray of a rainy day but the smoky gray of fog after rain. It fits his mother well. The boy wonders who paid for the dress. And then he detects a devilish smile hidden in the corners of L's lips. Of course L. is right there evaluating how his mother looks in the new dress. She nods in approval. She probably robbed the bank where she works to go around giving presents like that, the boy thinks.

Nex t L. tells the boy that she is inviting him to stay over in her house tonight. Her husband desperately needs a partner for a chess game. The boy is a good chess player – his uncles played with him back in Moscow when he was younger. They taught him all the fancy tricks. Well, her husband is nice. Good Lord, to be married to such a woman! Can you imagine? The boy feels a kind of solidarity with him. So he agrees for that one night.

But that night is only the beginning. Throughout the snowless winter and into the spring the boy is asked to play chess games many times. The boy is not stupid. He knows what it means: his mother is dating a man. The man's shadow is now everywhere – in numerous telephone calls from the man to the boy's house, in his mother's obnoxiously sweetened voice, in how she has allowed her hair to return to its natural color and then cut it short as fashion dictates. She looks like a tomboy. Other dresses follow that first gray one, and they are of brighter colors.

The boy is mysteriously silent, gulping away an enormous slice of apple pie at L.'s kitchen table. L. is on the phone. The boy's mother always says L. is gorgeous. This is strictly from a woman's point of view. The boy has known women who are far more beautiful: Wonder Woman, for instance. While he chews on the dough, he hears L.'s angry words, "No. No, you idiot. You can spoil everything. Tell him that until your relationship is dead serious you are not to present him to your son. You wait. Just be patient and follow what I tell you."

"Is it my Mama?" the boy asks. He is done with the pie and desperate for another helping, but he is not about to go through the humiliation of begging L. for another piece. L. does not answer his question but cuts a big slice of pie still warm and puts it on the boy's plate. Happily the boy sneaks bites of crust.

The boy stands outside L.'s house, a water pistol in his hand. L.'s dachshund is behind him. Under the blowing wind, each of them dreams of something different. The dachshund lifts its snout towards some noise. The boy turns to see a redheaded alien, a boy who is eyeing his water pistol.

"Hey," calls the redhead, "this pistol is mine. I lost one just like it an hour ago."

"Go away," says the boy.

"Come on, give me my gun," insists the stranger only a few inches taller.

Breathing hard, the dachshund looks up at the boy. The boy stays still.

The impossible stranger shouts, "You son-of-a-bitch, give me that gun." His hands aim for the boy. The dachshund, almost a puppy, gives a terrifying growl and opens his mouth ready to bite. The enemy runs off. Barking sharply, the dog chases the fleeing figure. After a short pursuit around the corner, the dog comes back, ears and tongue drooping. The boy returns to the house with the dog trotting along. Both are enveloped in gratified silence.

The moment comes. Suddenly the boy is able to be with L. without feeling raging anguish. She takes him to the exotic world of a local movie theater. The theater is full. The audience is noisy and restless. L.

and the boy take their seats in the first row. They are silent. The boy sits motionless throughout "Hair." The sound is stereophonic. On the way back home they howl into the air the tunes from the film. In L.'s bedroom they continue to shout melodies into the startled face of her husband.

Then it is July. The boy is in day camp, a combination of bus rides and suffocating games in an open field. The bus brings him home at three before his mother gets there from the English courses she is finally taking. The boy knows where the key is, though the door is never locked. He runs to the sink to get a handful of cold water. It is a hundred degrees outside. Inside the house it is a bit cooler, the small windows do not let the sun come in. The boy's forehead is damp. Sweat drops are all over his face. The telephone rings. The boy picks it up. It is a voice he is ready to acknowledge. His uncle Sergei inquires politely about his little pal's summer vacation – maybe together they can do something one day soon.

"Vacation is short. The camp is okay. Yes, it has a pool. I'm a very good swimmer. In fact, if you and I could drive to the ocean… No, nothing's new. The ocean is where I would like to swim, to jump over the waves, and after, we could build a sandcastle. No, everything's the same. Mama is getting married. A muddy castle decorated with towers and…Who? Them? Six months. The guy is okay. Where? How do I know? But listen, Sergei, why don't you call when Mama is here and tell her you and I are going to the ocean. Yeah, the guy is fine. Really, he is all right. Uh-huh. He is going to be my father, he told me. But the ocean… I'll tell her. The wedding? I don't know. Soon. Wait, she just walked in. Mama! Sergei is on the phone!"

His mother turns absolutely pale and starts to shiver. She takes the receiver into her trembling hands. She puts aside a year of cruel remarks and judgments, and through her dry mouth she says, "Hello, Sergei. I'm so happy you called. As a matter fact, I was thinking of calling you."

And through the entire afternoon as the boy contemplates dancing shadows on the TV screen, he is furious at his mother's loud voice interfering with the interesting programs.

"In the park," the boy hears his mother's happy talk. "Uh-huh…my friend, Mark calls her L., used her magnetic powers. She bewitched that man for me." She laughs. "Oh, we were introduced, stupid…"

The boy is full of self-respect as a result of his effort to appear compatible with his future father. Naturally, one could say that God wanted the match, and the boy just foresaw all of it coming. But he is glad that his fairy godmother was sent in the guise of a stranger. Having her near has some advantages: L. is the best cook in America…after his mother, that is.

A Secret

As to her beauty, I really do not know what to say, except that there was some, and yet there wasn't. It was so fleeting. Her depths were untouchable like the wind, her blue eyes could travel by themselves and attach to a wall or a tree, peering from there with intensity or languor. She would fall asleep wherever sleep caught up with her, then return from it without ever being surprised. Her character was a mystery to herself but left no trace of curiosity. I do remember cuts all over her arms, many small stamps of her anguish. "I'm thirsty," she would say kindly. Did she suffer? Who knows? The impression of her face was impersonal, eyes vacant as if there had been none of those macabre screams beforehand. Surely something was happening where she went from time to time, losing herself in the world of unreality. She came back to the surface with the same ignorance of which she did not speak but conveyed with a single glance under her short, clipped hair.

She was a patient with a face of serenity without any hope. And no one could take anything away from her—she was completely empty, but she had her own wisdom that she contained in a glass of water, in a crust of bread. Sketching, if someone paid attention, was something she learned when she traveled out of herself.

~

"Good afternoon," the woman in her thirties flashed her even white teeth at me. "Welcome to Bo Concept. My name is Natasha. I will be your interior designer." She extended her hand. "Talk to me. How can I help you?" Her long dark hair contrasted sharply with her blue eyes.

I said, "My name is Linda. I recently bought an apartment—two bedrooms, living, dining, kitchen, three bathrooms. You know, the whole shebang. And I have no idea what to do with it. I want something modern, light …" I interrupted myself. "Where did you study interior design?"

Natasha brought her hands up to pull her hair back. The sleeves of her white silk blouse rolled up to her elbows. Cuts! I recognized the scars. Many years ago when I interned at a private mental hospital just for a month on rotation, I became fascinated with a young woman about seventeen years old brought there by a monstrous-looking older man who never showed up again. Someone paid for her stay. She was so indifferent to the world around her. She wasn't sad or scared or rebellious. Her frozen-like features showed no desperation. Uninterested, apathetic. Brought to the suicide ward after she had been discovered cutting herself.

This woman, Natasha, sitting across the desk, cloaked in self-sufficiency, sure of herself, full lips covered with ruby lipstick, was anything but the outline of that sick girl of long ago. This creature had wings, or so she wanted you to believe.

"Natasha," I said, "you don't remember me. I was one of the interns who observed you at the psychiatric institution. A very unappetizing-looking man brought you there. I was even a little scared. What an unexpected meeting! So happy to see you."

Natasha's fingers clung to her neck. "We have a guest, Richard," she said in a low voice to an approaching man. Her face significantly paled.

Richard nodded "Hello" to me and turned to Natasha. His brow knitted. "Are you all right?"

Natasha got up. "I need a glass of water," she said and walked away.

"She is pregnant," Richard whispered. "But the thing is, she shouldn't be. Apparently, she is very fragile, and the doctors told her not to get pregnant. Natasha, as stubborn as she was, disobeyed, and I don't know how all of this is going to end." Richard slumped into an empty chair next to mine. "Of course, to me she is a robust, healthy woman who for some reason was instructed by doctors not to have children and she doesn't want to get married."

"Married to you?" I allowed myself a question as if we were intimate friends.

"Yes," he said, "to me. She is full of secrets and mysteries, but I love her. I was her teacher at the Corcoran School of Art and Design. She sort of looked like all the girls – tee-shirt, jeans, sneakers, except she was very different." He thought for a moment. "And her designs were different. Enigmatic, minimalistic, and kind of foreign, as if taken from a different planet." He looked at me. "I know very little about her past. She told me she came from Russia to study here. And that's about it. She's been working for me here at the store since her graduation."

I felt stuffed with all this information and memories of a younger Natasha.

Richard continued. "She makes good money here. People trust her taste. How could they not? She has so many ideas. I don't know where she gets them. They're so original."

I opened my mouth. A suggestive answer was ripening on my tongue, as I noticed Natasha's white blouse outlining her swollen breasts. She was coming back looking straight at me with familiar disaffected glance that I understood was a sign. She was giving me a warning, calling me to be silent.

I looked at my watch, mumbled some excuse and left the store, never to return.

The Gulag Archipelago

"Yes, I am Maria Rubin. Boris Rubin? Yes, he lives here. He's my husband. Only he's not home now, already left for work. Oh, you want to talk to me? Okay. What is this about? In private? I should come to you? Where? Yes, I know that building. Everyone knows that mysterious building – it's the KGB headquarters, if I understand correctly. What does it have to do with me? Just for a friendly talk? What about?" Maria glanced at her three-month-old son, peacefully snoozing in his crib. She knew that under his lids his eyes were cobalt blue like her husband's, and for some reason she took special pride in that. "When? Now? But I have a baby. I really can't." She closed her eyes. "Is it that important? At 10 o'clock?" Maria looked at her watch. It was 9. The mysterious voice sounded insistent. "Well, if you put it that way, I'll think of something. Yes, I know, it's three blocks from where I am. Room 222? Whom should I ask for?"

"Maria," Maria's mother, who came to help on her day off, walked out from the kitchen with an iron in her hand. "Who's calling you? If you need to go anywhere, I'll stay with Mark." Rich aroma from freshly baked piroshki broke into the one-room apartment.

"Okay," Maria said into the receiver, "I'll be there at 10." Her heart in her throat, she hung up the receiver with trembling hands.

"Honey, go, do whatever you need to do. Mark will be fine."

Maria mouthed, "Thank you," and moved closer to the crib. She was thinking she should really wake him up to feed him before she left. But then, again, who knows how long this visit was going to last? Maybe forever. She shivered. She could not part with her son. "You know what, Mom? I'll take Mark with me. He needs fresh air. It was Olga on the phone asking me to help her with the dress she is making for her wedding. She's so excited, I couldn't say no."

"Of course, sweetheart. Go. I will finish ironing diapers and go home. Imagine, it's 1973 and we're still boiling and ironing diapers. In the West, I've heard, diapers are disposable." Her mom danced back into the kitchen humming a popular tune.

Maria swaddled Mark in layers of blankets, put him in a carriage, and covered him with yet another blanket. The December weather was not exactly welcoming. Mark was not bothered by all the fuss and continued to sleep peacefully. Three blocks and fifteen minutes later, Maria forced herself through a massive door into a vast marble vestibule of KGB headquarters. In a tall dark mirror, she saw herself as an insignificant speck that could be easily removed with the slight flick of someone's finger. Underneath her winter coat, her flannel shirt was soaked in sweat.

A militia man asked, "How may I help you?"

She straightened. "I'm here to see Lieutenant Berdeyev."

As she exited the elevator on the second floor, a young pretty girl ushered Maria, all the way her eyebrows raised in disbelief as if to say, a baby in a carriage, really! A dark brown wooden door opened, and in a room with a very high ceiling, a man in uniform came closer, smiling kindly. "Hello, hello. Who do we have here? A boy? Mark? A great name, almost like Karl Marx." He laughed. "Maria, I take it. Sit down. Make yourself comfortable. Would you like some tea? It's cold outside." He pushed the button on his phone. "Tatyana, darling, organize some tea for us. Quickly." He looked at Maria almost fatherly. "We don't want to take a lot of your time, obviously. So let's get to it right away while your Mark is asleep."

"I apologize," said Maria. "There was no one to leave him with, so…"

"Don't worry about it. I understand. I'm a parent too. It's not easy." He touched the rim of his glasses with his pudgy hand. "We're not interested in you, Maria. You're fine. It's your husband who concerns us." He fell silent for a moment, as if recalling something. "Yes, he, Boris is one of my concerns, as he should be yours as well."

Tatyana brought in tea and biscuits on a tray and left.

"Eat, eat, dear. You're a nursing mother. Are you nursing?"

"Yes," Maria whispered. She was losing her strength.

"Anyway," the lieutenant straightened his shoulders and continued in a more assertive voice, "your husband delivers anti-Soviet speeches messing with the heads of his colleagues at work. We received signals from those people who work with him, and they are very discontent." The lieutenant gulped his tea. "Oh, that's so good – Georgian tea, no less. They are our friends." Maria did not attempt to pick up her cup, fearing that she would not be able to hold it. "Your husband also was convincing those people to read certain forbidden literature, offering them manuscripts he is obtaining from the West! From our enemies!" The Lieutenant coughed with anger. His eyes narrowed as he got up, agitated. All his previous courtesy vanished. "You, Maria, as a wife, most likely know everything. You must tell me the absolute truth, or…" He shook his finger at Maria's face.

Maria offered in a trembling voice, "I don't know anything, Comrade Berdeyev. My husband is not involved in anything criminal or unlawful. He is a simple draughtsman and a father. She looked at Mark, who had started fidgeting, most likely because of the heat in the room or the lieutenant's loud voice.

"Well?" The lieutenant looked at Maria, menacingly pointing his fist with his knuckles turning white. There was not a trace of his recent sweetness in his voice. "We will have to search your apartment and see for ourselves how 'innocent' you are."

Maria lifted her eyes filled with terror. "When?"

"Now," barked the lieutenant. He picked up a cigarette from a pack on his desk and lit it. Maria noticed *Marlboro* written on the pack, an incredible luxury in the Soviet Union. He opened the door. "Tatyana, get dressed, and tell Pavel to join. You are going to escort this woman to her house and look for whatever inappropriate material they have there." He turned his head to Maria. "Go. Don't forget your offspring." He slightly pushed the carriage. Maria rolled the carriage out of the room. The door noisily shut behind her.

Tatyana and a man, both in uniforms, were awaiting her. On the way home, she thought that she might not make it and fall down, her knees were so weak. In her inner eye, she could see one thing and one thing only – a large manuscript of Solzhenitsyn's *The Gulag Archipelago* sitting on her coffee table covered with *Pravda*, the governmental newspaper. She had covered the manuscript with *Pravda* to hide it from her mother. It had been the quickest thing to do when her mother rang the bell. But of course, these two in uniforms will remove *Pravda* and discover the manuscript, a death sentence or years in prison for her husband.

Maria had read the underground publication her husband brought home. It was a document of the atrocities done in the series of camps under the general name of Gulag to political prisoners and ordinary criminals sentenced there to forced labor. The book showed the treatment of prisoners, their inhuman living conditions, some specific events – rebellions and uprisings – the cruelty of it all. Solzhenitsyn was aware that after Khrushchev's 1956 speech denouncing Stalins personality cult, many practices in those camps had been stopped. But the basic structure of the system survived and could be revived. Never before had Maria met with the horrors of the Gulag. *It had all happened in real life*, she thought, *as real as what was happening now*. She could barely breathe.

As she and her convoy entered her small apartment, Maria felt temporary relief that her mother was gone. *Pravda* was where she had left it. Tatyana and Pavel immediately started the search even before taking off their coats. Pavel went straight to the kitchen, Tatyana to the bathroom. The loud noises from the opening and closing of cupboards, drawers, the medicine cabinet, trash cans, heavy steps, coughing woke up Mark, who immediately started to scream. Maria unwrapped him. The stench from his poop rose into the air. Maria changed him, but that didn't stop Mark from carrying on. "Hungry," she sighed. Pavel and Tatyana returned to the room.

"I have found nothing," Pavel said and wrinkled his nose. "You?"

"Nothing," said Tatyana.

"Let's frisk this room before I die from this stink,"

Tatyana looked at Maria. "If you need to feed him, do."

Maria took off her coat, sweater, and unbuttoned her blouse.

"It doesn't bother us," Pavel said and winked at Tatyana. They continued to tap under the mattress, through away the linen and pillows from the bed, turned over everything inside Mark's crib. Mark quieted down and was sucking at his mother's breast with obvious joy. The tram behind their first-floor window rang passing by. Maria remembered that there was another life outside her walls. *God have mercy on us*, she prayed silently.

Mark weakened his grip, satisfied and smiling. Maria raised him up and burped him on the back. Pavel and Tatyana finished with the rest of the room and came closer to the coffee table where Maria was standing with Mark in her arms. At this moment Mark burped and a huge white ribbon of milk gagged out of his mouth and fell on *Pravda*, covering it with vomit. "Oh, my God," exclaimed Maria. "I'm sorry. I'm so sorry. I'll clean up."

"Don't worry, Comrade," Pavel said. "We understand. Take care of your baby. Tatyana, let's go."

They left leaving a suffocating odor behind them. It took the entire afternoon to get rid of it.

Years later, Mark when scolded by his wife for something he had forgotten to do, to buy, to get, always told her, "Be quiet, woman! I saved my father's life even before you were born." She was a whole six months younger than him.

A Winning

My story is about how suddenly, unexpectedly, against all odds, we became rich. As a family, Papa, Mama, and I— we were often presented as friendly, quiet, and uninventive. I was usually satisfied with such an introduction. Perhaps it was a lack of imagination. Though at the same time I was dreaming of seeing the Atlantic Ocean or Mediterranean Sea, an absurd fantasy that lay deep inside of me as a dark secret. Papa was a doctor, Mama was an accountant at a public school, and I at twenty-three was still the centerpiece of their existence. We confronted money problems from the end of the month until the next salary payment was received, when life would reconfigure itself again from worries into something slightly less troubling.

I was finishing my studies at Moscow State University with no prospect of work or marriage. I reminded myself of a piece of driftwood floating down the river with no aim, goal, consequence, or care. People around me had started disappearing, as if sucked into desert sand that covered them completely. The Soviet Union had opened the coveted gate to the West for those who had or claimed to have relatives in Israel, and the attraction to escape had become contagious. After decades, being an unfortunate Jew was finally paying off. Only Jewish brains were allowed to leave the country. We could leave—we were Jews—but we continued to confront money problems. Emigration required plenty more. One had to pay for airplane tickets, for the official refusal of Soviet citizenship, for having received higher education, for bribes (oh, the infatuation with bribes in Moscow!), and for much more. We felt left behind because of our inability to meet the requirements. Our moral enthusiasm had started to extinguish like an abandoned bonfire, and all that was left was a flickering light, sort of "it would have been nice, but …"

But back to my story. It was an ordinary Sunday morning with the aroma of my mother's pancakes, my father's usual lying on the couch in his pajamas, newspaper in his hands, and my hanging out without much to do. Suddenly my father made a funny face and looked at me over his glasses, asking me to come closer, his voice feeble and shaking. "Look!" he said pointing at some numbers in the newspaper.

I read "593471." While I was reading, my father was breathing down my neck.

"Now look at this." He handed me a crumbled bond receipt. "Read it out loud."

"593471——What does it mean?" I asked.

He snatched the bond receipt from my hand. Investments in government bonds in the Soviet Union were like buying lottery tickets. "That means …Alisa!" he roared. My mother ran from the kitchen with a knife in her hand. My father jumped off the couch and rolling his eyes toward the ceiling, declared, "I need a cigar!"

"You don't smoke. What is all this?" My mother stared at him.

"Friends, family, comrades, people, you won't believe what just happened. The Messiah just entered the room and set his blessing on us! We won 5,000 rubles!" He brushed his hair with his fingers as if to look appropriate for the benefit of his invisible benefactor. "My dearest friends, do you understand what this means?"

Simultaneously my father screamed "A Volga car!" and my mother yelled "Emigration!"

My mother's eyes rounded and looked as if they were ready to tumble from their sockets with deadly surprise at my father's choice for our future. My father coughed in confusion and indignation.

"Emigration? Kiss my ass. We need to live a little bit, to have some pleasure." He grabbed my mother by her shoulders and shook her. "Do you understand? 5,000 rubles! We're able to afford a Volga, the best car there is. I'll tell you what – I will let you choose the color." We knew my father had been passionate about cars all his life, recognizing all the Soviet and foreign models, spending hours reading automobile manuals, freezing on the street while admiring a particular car that had just passed by. One time our family visited an exhibition of foreign cars, and my father just stared and stared at them like a child fascinated by shiny unattainable toys.

"Listen, comrades, my loved ones—you know I love you and want the best for you, don't

you? Our neighbor Gosha is selling his Volga for only 4,500. It's almost brand new. We will even have some money left for a new—I don't know —a rug, a bed, clothes, whatever. Gosha, the 'freedom-fighter' for blue jeans got an exit visa and is running away, but we …" —he looked with pride at my mother and me— "We are not running anywhere! We are better than that. We are thinkers. We will take the time to think things through. But while we are doing so, we will have a Volga. Oh my God, people, be reasonable!" He almost broke down crying.

My mother and I were paralyzed with despair stuck between our dream and my father's. We were all silent for a while. Finally, my father's arms sort of fell by his sides like deflated balloons. He looked at us and said, "I need to take a shower." He was indeed kind of sweaty at that moment. "Listen, forget about the car. We'll pay for exit visas and everything else and leave." His voice was completely dead. My mother's eyes settled on my father's silly mess of hair and said, "No, you forget it. We'll buy a car."

My father's bent over figure straightened up. "But you said …"

"I changed my mind." My mother looked at me. "We changed our minds. You are right. We will have a car and a whole new wardrobe and …"

"No, no, no!" My father was shaking his head. "I know what the two of you really want, and

I …"

"Oh," my mother smiled, "you just wanted to be a hero. And we won't let you." She picked up the paper. "Give me the lucky bond number. I just want to see it with my own eyes." My mother dealt with numbers all day long at work. She scanned the bond with her eyes and then glanced at the newspaper. Her eyes began to twinkle. She came up to me and embraced me with one arm and wrapped the other around my father. "You two," she said, dying from laughter, "are such idiots. The number 1 of the bond is a 4 in the newspaper. I guess there wasn't enough ink to make it clear."

Indeed, it appeared our family was saved.

A Thank-You Note

"But in any event, my intentions were purely noble. Besides, I cannot tell a lie – you know that."

"I don't know that. I…"

At this moment, as Ralph and Greta approached their destination, a white two-story house off Connecticut Avenue, a cocker spaniel met them at the entrance door barking loudly and wiggling his tail with an intensity that indicated overflowing joy at their appearance. Why? Who knows. It was its nature, or its masters were nice to it. Washington, D.C., contained all sorts of people – a melting pot of a town.

"Come in, come in." A maid in a uniform ushered them into the house.

Greta and Ralph entered a vast living-dining room and immediately lost each other among the loudly talking, moving crowd that was consuming alcohol and Russian caviar glistening in several jars next to a mayonnaise crab salad, steamed lobster tails, and a long stretch of baked salmon decorated with roasted almonds, all set on a long oval table. Greta was not fond of the business soirées of her husband's organization, the Smithsonian, events where she knew almost no one, but Ralph had begged her to attend. Her immediate feelings were to get out of there as soon as possible. On a background of uniformly black dresses, she, in a short green number, looked like someone's mistress.

After she tasted the caviar - too salty - and the salmon - too raw - with a gentle swinging gait she approached Ralph. He was involved in conversation with a woman who looked somewhat familiar. Gracefully Greta asked him to take her home. "I have a terrible headache," she grimaced.

Greta recognized the woman almost immediately. It was whom Greta and her husband Ralph had been talking about on the way to the party. Ralph had asked Greta if she had sent a thank-you note to the renowned aging scholar and his wife, for dinner at their house. Greta recalled the evening, a gloomy affair, the frozen air of the dark room interrupted only by the husband's passionate monologue involving a book that he had just published about species that disappeared a million years ago. Greta had not listened. "What a pompous bore," she had thought. She had observed the space around her in which books dominated any other furnishings. Now, Greta had nothing against books. She herself had been teaching art at an elementary school. But she was against self-promotion and hunger. She had begun to feel really hungry. Soon Greta and Ralph had been offered water and popcorn. The evening lasted in this manner for about two and a half hours. Greta incessantly yawned. No one had addressed her once, not even her husband who was intently nodding his head listening to the old man. When they finally had left, Greta breathed deeply several times to relieve her anger. She had not wanted to upset her husband, who was enthusiastically talking about how smart the old man was. "Please write them a thank-you note," he had casually said to Greta. She had not responded.

Tonight on the way to this evening's soirée, Ralph, excited as he always was before such occasions, said, "By the way, there are going to be some people you know. Remember the couple who cordially invited us to their home for dinner, the world-known scholar and his wife? Did you send them a thank-you note?" Ralph slowed his step for a moment.

"Of course, darling," said Greta. "Nothing to worry about. I sent one the very next day."

Reassured, Ralph smiled with satisfaction. "I'm glad we brought them flowers then, not wine. What did you write in it, dear?"

Greta squinted at the pollen falling from the blossoming cherry trees, a specialty of Washington, D.C., that attracted tourists from all over. "Wine would have been a better choice in my opinion. Well, never mind. I wrote 'Thank you very much for a lovely evening, but I'd rather be fucking…'"

"Not funny." Ralph looked at her severely. "Tell me the truth, what did you write?"

Greta shrugged her shoulders. "That's exactly what I wrote. I'm sorry if you disapprove, but my intentions were purely noble…" And then the cocker spaniel ended their discussion by greeting them at the door with loud barks. Otherwise Greta would have told Ralph that of course she was joking, that she had sent a boring Hallmark thank-you card, a few banalities written by an idiot, and had just signed it for them both.

As Ralph, after seeing the pleading in Greta's eyes to leave the party, excused himself and they entered the chilly air of the quiet city, Greta said, "What did you talk about with this awful woman who has the social graces of a dried herring? "

"A very inaccurate description," Ralph grunted.

"Whatever." Greta rolled her eyes.

"Well, first I asked how her husband was. I had heard that he is not well. And then I apologized for your rude, inappropriate thank-you note and begged her forgiveness for the unfortunate incident. The poor woman didn't know what to say, she looked totally confused."

Greta's laughter of epic proportions seemed to be able to wake up the perfect order of the street on which their car was parked. She thought that this might be the most appropriate moment to tell Ralph she was pregnant.

A Chance

"Hang on. Hang on a little more. Everything is going to be alright." Nadia was ordering herself to stay positive, but her entire body was trembling on this hot, polluted Moscow August day.

The events of yesterday flashed in her head like movie scenes – a crowded hall of Moscow University with applicants, a vision of excitement and agitation, filling out the necessary papers. A hope in everyone's eyes, including hers, she imagined. A cup of strong coffee in her shaking hand had spilled onto the floor, and she was afraid to look around to see if anyone had noticed. Her own daring had been rising with every passing minute. Nadia Krasovskaya, she wrote, using her mom's last name that sounded more Russian than her dad's, Zimmerman, which was clearly Jewish. She knew enough about camouflaged antisemitism in the Soviet Union not to disclose her parents' and her origin. Then came the questions of age – eighteen; gender - female; place of birth – Moscow; Date of birth – May 19, 1950; address and telephone number; and finally glaring as a nasty punishment, nationality.

Nadia had bitten her lip and gazed at the paper. If she would write "Jew" as in her passport, she might as well get up and leave and continue with the kind of life that was permitted to her. She could enter a less prestigious school and become a teacher, a nurse, or an accountant. At the same time, graduates of Moscow University's Division of Foreign Affairs and Diplomacy would be working with foreigners, enjoying all sorts of privileges – foreign cigarettes, chewing gum, coveted business trips to the West. But for Jews, defined as potential enemies of the state, it was taboo. This notion caused discomfort but not outrage in Nadia. She was more ashamed of being a Jew than concerned with the injustice being practiced. In the blank for nationality, she wrote "Russian."

From where she was standing now, still trembling, she continued to look at the building across the street, her dream university. It seemed enormous, unattainable, never to be a part of her world. She knew very well why the idea of breaking through the impossible had become so irresistible. They had been dancing, dancing, dancing, with candles flickering all around. Fast quirky rock 'n roll, slow melancholy blues, their faces close to each other, his and hers. He was a tall, moneyed guy, the grandson of someone very, very important. Almost biting her ear, he whispered hotly, "I hate all those minorities – Georgians, Armenians, Jews…" Nadia had stiffened inside hoping that he would not recognize that she was one of those people. He didn't. He held her tight. She enjoyed leaning against him with her shapely curves. He boasted, "I study diplomacy at the University. It's fucking grand. What about you?" He kissed her.

It was one of those anonymous parties that brought them together. Nadia knew almost no one. A spasm of anxiety had crossed her face. Her lips said "I will start the University in September. I'm sure I will be admitted."

"Don't be so sure," he laughed. "But you could mention my name, Semichastny. My grandfather is the Chairman of the KGB."

Nadia, in shock from her audacity at having lied in her application, still turned it in. A girl in dark clothes, her face showing not a single emotion as if she had died a long time ago with ridiculously thick eyebrows, an exact copy of Brezhnev's who had just come to power, glanced at Nadia's application form and said, "Passport."

"What?"

"You want the pass for the entrance exams?"

"Yes."

"Then show me your passport."

Nadia expressed serious surprise. "I'm sorry. I didn't bring it. I didn't know. I…"

"Bring the passport tomorrow. The exams start in two days. Don't hold up the line. Next!"

"What about the pass for the exams?"

"Didn't you hear me? When you show me your passport, I'll give you your pass."

Nadia had the exact number of coins for the bus to take her home. But she decided to walk, tears running down her cheeks. Forget the elite school, forget the lucrative future jobs, visits to foreign countries. Forget Paris, Berlin, Warsaw. Semichastny's grandson had not called her. She should study medicine or become a librarian. She so much wanted to step up, to reach the unreachable. She wiped the tears from her face, thinking if only she could wipe the Jewishness off her as easily.

"I'll do anything for you,." her friend had said when Nadia approached her in the morning. "I mean, I think it's crazy. Why do you even want to join those snobs? You're better than them or that stupid, pompous university."

"Listen, if you don't want to do it, if you're scared or something…then don't. I understand."

"That's not what I said. Okay, give me your dress and what else? Your scarf? Well, do I look like you?"

"You look exactly like me, only a Russian version of me with your blue eyes, blonde braids, and the like."

They stared at the mirror – same height, same build. They laughed. "So, remember!" Nadia said to the reflection of her friend. "The most important thing is the passport. The passport! It's in the pocket of the dress you're wearing. Go to the admission table, give them my application, and ask for a pass to the exams. If the zombie bitch asks for a passport, just show it to her. And if she asks why on the application you are Russian but in the passport Jewish, say, 'Oh my God! I filled out the application for a friend who is sick. I didn't know she is Jewish.' Say you are sorry and just leave. I'll wait for you outside. But the chances are that you look so Russian, she won't even ask for a passport and will give you a pass for the exams. And then…"

Nadia looked at her watch. Only ten minutes had passed since her friend had entered the building. If the plan she had so brilliantly concocted worked, Nadia would be able to take the exams. She was not worried about the exams – she had prepared and was sure she would pass. I don't need Semichastny's name, she told herself. Besides, he is really ugly. He looks like one of those Nazis they show in the movies with watery eyes and mean mouth. What right does he have to hate Georgians, Armenians, Jews, and others? He is sick. I hate him. I truly do. And that bitch who sits at the admission table is sick too. She is a part of the system, with no brains. I am sure she hates Jews just as much. She looks like Cerberus, the dog who guards the gate to Hell. Exactly. Hell is what it is. Do I want to belong to that evil machine with an appetite for destruction and humiliation? Do I want to become Kafka's Josef K.? Under her breath she recited the first line of The Trial that she had recently read: "Somebody must have made a false accusation against Josef K., for he was arrested one morning without having done anything wrong." The nature of my crime is being a Jew, Nadia thought. Her pulse was racing. But her shivering stopped. She straightened her shoulders.

"Hey!" her friend appeared on the other side of the street. "Let me tell you what happened."

Nadia waved her hand. "Come on over here. Whatever. I don't care anymore. I'm an idiot." She looked at the burning sky. "Let's go get some ice cream."

Ballet Slippers

Mia's stifled laughter was brought about not by anything funny but by hatred. She was absorbed in the rather unambitious, stupid activity of splashing the dirty water in a puddle with her brand new black glossy shoes and snow-white socks. No one was around, and the private show was meant for the enemy who lived in her head – her stepmother Miranda.

Miranda had come into Mia's life unannounced one warm evening in the beginning of the summer. For three months Mia had tolerated Miranda's meddling in her and her father's lives, but this morning Miranda had overstepped all boundaries. She had walked into Mia's room with a box tied with a pink ribbon and put it next to Mia's bed. "This is for you, for your first day of school. You'll be like everyone else."

Everyone else starts school at age seven, Mia thought, *and I am eight.* Because of her mother's death a year ago, her consequent hospitalization with pneumonia, her father's being a wreck, and no one else around, Mia had spent three months in the hospital. Her father said it was a blessing, since it gave him time to organize their lives. He worked as a car mechanic, and when Mia was discharged from the hospital, she hung around the garage where he worked for long hours and afterwards went home together with him. Both ate cereal with milk and collapsed into sleep.

When her mother had been alive, everything had been different. Every day had been magic – her mother had made it feel that way. They rode bikes, played badminton, occasionally took a local train from Jamaica, New York where they lived, to the countryside to collect butterflies and leaves of different shapes and colors. Although Mia's mother had always been physically weak, she was very energetic like a child wishing to experience life to its fullest as if she knew her time was short, and she had to hurry.

With the arrival of this strange new woman Miranda, Mia, seeing creams and lotions and perfumes her mother had never used, was outraged. Miranda's underwear hung in the bathroom alongside other pieces of clothing. To Mia it looked scandalous. Was it jealousy, this hatred? Was it grief? Was it growing up? Miranda begged her to eat the meals she had cooked, but Mia only showed disgust.

"The girl's in trouble," she heard Miranda say to her father.

"She just misses her mom," he murmured. "Give it some time. She had a special relationship with her mom. It will pass."

"You're indulging her," Miranda replied.

What does this stupid Miranda understand? The ballet slippers were Mom's, and she gave them to me since she couldn't dance any longer. So what that they're too big for me. It's nice to wear them to bed even. This way Mom is with me all the time.

Miranda was adamant about replacing the ballet slippers with "appropriate" shoes for Mia.

When her father had brought Miranda into their family, he had said, "Mia, this is Miranda. She is going to take care of us."

Miranda had approached her and said with pity, "You poor girl. I'm going to look after you. Do you like to paint?"

Mia had stopped breathing. "Go away!" Tears gushed from her eyes, and she ran to her room.

"She will come around," she heard her father say.

"Then there's no problem," Miranda concluded.

Everything was quiet for a while. Then one day Miranda said, "How long are you going to wear those ridiculous ballet slippers? Never mind that girls do not wear those to school…"

"I'm not replacing them with anything! Do not touch them!" Mia roared.

This morning Mia had awakened to a strange sensation: her feet were bare. She searched around with her eyes. There were no ballet slippers anywhere. Instead there was old ugly (definitely older than mom) Miranda with a box inside of which, when Mia looked, were black shiny shoes with white socks stuck in them. This turned Mia into an animal. She appeared in the kitchen barefoot, her face distorted in rage.

"Did you brush your teeth?" Miranda asked calmly. "Your Dad's already gone to work. Breakfast is on the table. Do you want me to take you to school? It's your first day."

Mia did not even look at the food. "Where are my slippers?!"

"I put them away for now. I guess you don't want me to take you to school. Okay, then go by yourself. Just don't be late. Thankfully the school is around the corner."

Back from school after Mia enthusiastically had killed the particles of sun reflected in the puddle and had practically ruined her new shoes and socks, for which she felt no guilt, she entered her dilapidated building and, skipping steps, tried to reach her apartment on the second floor.

She had always resented sullen strangers. Mom had disliked them and had told her to avoid contact with them. One such stranger was standing on the landing between the first and second floors, smiling at her with his toothless mouth. "Come closer, little girl. How old are you?" Something in his eyes was not right. It brewed danger.

"Eleven," lied Mia, hoping to scare him.

One of his hands held what looked like a large piece of raw meat sticking out of his unzipped pants. He chuckled. "Do you like chocolate? Come and taste it. It's the best chocolate you've ever had." He grabbed her with his other hand by the sleeve of her shirt and pulled her close to him. The stench from whatever it was in his hand was unbearable. Mia in shock started screaming as he pushed her head down. "Shut up, little whore! Just try it, you'll love it." Mia bit her sharp little teeth into his hand that was pulling her toward him. He moaned in pain. "You bitch, I'm going to…"

At this moment they both heard a scream, "What? You sick bastard, let go of my daughter! I'm going to have you arrested!" Miranda, in a state of absolute horror, thrust a bag full of groceries onto the stranger's head. The eggs in it broke and covered him with their yolks from head to toe while Miranda repeatedly punched him with her fists. "You pig! You belong in a mental institution! You're the scum of the earth!" But he was already gone.

Miranda looked at Mia's face and then down at the muddy, soiled, stained, wet shoes Mia was wearing.

"Sorry," said Mia, following Miranda's eyes.

"I'm sorry too. I will put your ballet slippers back into your room, sweetheart."

"Thank you," said Mia. They embraced and remained like that for a long time.

Mary

"Mary, darling, you're the best nurse I've ever met." Mr. Buono was sitting on the edge of his bed.

"Oh, thank you, Mr. Buono, you're the best patient I've ever met. Here is water and another cup with all your pills. Swallow them." She handed both cups to him.

"I will swallow anything you give me, Mary. But beforehand I must tell you that you are not only the most beautiful nurse I have ever seen but also the best singer I have ever heard. Last night at the staff concert you sang so gorgeously, I felt as if I were transported into a universe of angels."

"Oh, you're too nice, Mr. Buono."

"No, no, your voice is one of a kind. Where did you learn to sing like that? Did you study voice?"

"I didn't. I wanted to, but my mama kept saying I had no talent in that regard, that it would be more practical to learn one of the medical professions so that eventually I could earn a living and support myself. So I did as mama said, and here I am. I like what I'm doing. Singing was great, but it was one of those sweet dreams, certainly unrealistic."

"But Mary! Please excuse me for meddling in your affairs, but sweetheart, you are a talent. A real talent, if I may say so myself, having been a choir boy in a church chorus some years ago in Philadelphia. It's a great city for singers. There's this one place, the best, where people study voice. I forget the name, but you can look it up." Mr. Buono smoothed out his plaid shirt, thinking that he should have worn his fresh white one.

"I have to go, Mr. Buono." Mary smiled and gathered her equipment – blood pressure monitor, stethoscope, thermometer. Mr. Buono decided that it was a sufficiently meaningful smile she gave him, and the question in his mind about Mary's feelings towards him was drifting in a positive direction.

"Will I see you tomorrow, Mary?" Mr. Buono's heart was swelling from a secret emotion.

"No," said Mary. "Did you forget, Mr. Buono? Tomorrow is Monday, my day off."

"Anything special planned?"

"Not really," said Mary on her way out. "Probably the beach as usual in the summer in Miami. Too hot to do anything else."

Mr. Buono felt a pang of jealousy. "Alone?"

"Mr. Buono, behave. Take all your pills and rest. After all, even though mild, your stroke was a serious thing. You take care of yourself, and you'll be running to the beach as well in no time."

"Sing me something, Mary."

Mary laughed and flew away in a sudden rush.

The next day, Monday, was going slow: a doctor's visit for a few minutes, a half hour of physical therapy, some boring meals they called "healthy." Mr. Buono's wife was away at her sister's somewhere in New Jersey. Mr. Buono didn't care. After all, she was still young and mobile, barely seventy, twelve years younger than he was. The rehabilitation center had a good reputation for taking care of their patients, still his wife was usually bringing him his favorite dried fruits and chocolate, and he was kind of missing her.

Another patient from the room next to Mr. Buono's peered through the door. "Hi, pal."

"Oh, good morning, neighbor. Come in, come in."

"It's not morning. It's late afternoon."

"Who cares? Sit down. Tell me, did you enjoy the concert the other day? I'm still thinking about it. I enjoyed it a lot. Our nurse, Mary, was so good, wasn't she? I told her she sang beautifully, like a nightingale."

"You did? I'm not an expert, but she was awful, couldn't even carry a tune. She's a good-looking gal, shapely, but singing?"

Mr. Buono seemed a bit unhappy. "Why, I told her she was the star."

"The star? Are you deaf?" The neighbor eyed the open jar of cherry jam on the table, but Mr. Buono did not offer it to him.

Mr. Buono sighed. "Yes, I am deaf. That evening I forgot my hearing aid." He became sad faced. "I will tell her the truth tomorrow when she comes. I will apologize. I'll explain everything." He swallowed nervously several times.

Mary did not come the next day or the following. Mr. Buono was sinking into his regular depression. Finally when Friday came and Mary had still not shown up, Mr. Buono anxiously asked another nurse who came with his pills, "Is Mary alright? Where is she? Why hasn't she come to work for almost a week?"

"Mary? The young girl? She's strange. She gave one day notice for no apparent reason. Her mother called and said that suddenly her daughter had packed up and left for Philadelphia. Some fool here told her that she has a singing talent. I have to tell you, Mr. Buono, she's as terrible as a rooster early in the morning. But she believed that fool. They say that there's some sort of Academy of Vocal Arts in Philadelphia for the super-duper-talented, and that's where she went. Mr. Buono, are you alright?"

On the Brooklyn-Queens Expressway

"Fuck the natural hair, dark, frizzy and dull." Kate glanced at a car mirror, her hair now was blonde, slick and shiny. "Thank God for hot irons." She frowned. "Will he recognize me? It's been twelve years since we saw each other last."

This New York Friday was hot and humid, but inside her air-conditioned Mercedes SUV, she felt comfortably cool. The traffic moved slowly. The Brooklyn-Queens Expressway was packed. She looked in the rear mirror and could still see the Verrazano bridge she had just crossed driving from New Jersey. JFK Airport was still some distance away.

If for some strange reason a reporter would be interviewing her now, asking questions about her life, she would have no answers. Yesterday she was sure of her position in life – a mother to a five-year-old girl, a wife, a homemaker, a poetry-writer, a published poetry writer at that. But now?

Her friend Amelia had called at the romantic hour of 6:30 a.m. when it was still dark outside, waking her up. Her husband's empty place in bed reminded her that he was away on a business trip. The door to her daughter's bedroom was shut tight, not a sound. The house made her feel at peace – it always had that effect on her. She picked up the thundering telephone. "Kate, Kate!" Amelia's voice delivered clashing emotions of *Sorry, I called so early* and *what I'm going to tell you couldn't wait*. "Sergei is coming. He's flying from some kind of mathematics conference in L.A. with a three-hour layover in New York, after which he will fly back home to Moscow. He wants to see us," Amelia blurted all of it in one breath.

"Who is us?" By minimizing the number of words, Kate hoped that Amelia would not detect how in one blow she had turned Kate's world upside-down.

"Me and Misha, of course. His best friend."

"Did he mention my name?"

"No."

In a matter of seconds Kate limited her turmoil to a specific decision. She would drive to the airport and face Sergei in person. "What time did you say he is landing?"

"10:30 a.m. at JFK. You're not going to show up, are you?" Amelia whispered.

Kate looked at her wristwatch: 6:45 a.m. At 7:30 she would wake up her daughter. At 8:15 the school bus would come to pick her up. Then she would have time to take a shower, dress, and go. Her husband would never know. Besides, is it really a crime to see your ex-flame who lives in Moscow and never once contacted her in the twelve years since she left the Soviet Union in 1987. Sergey had taken her to Sheremetyevo Airport after she received her exit visa, repeated that he was not ready for such a big step, kissed her goodbye and left. She was very hurt. "No complaints to the universe now," she thought. "Everything's fine. I'm just interested in archeology."

The size of her car did not allow Kate to maneuver easily through the heavy traffic. She felt a bit suffocated as if she were in deep water and a heavy current was pushing her in a direction she did not want to go.

She remembered how Sergei had appeared from nowhere. Her life had been sort of slow without him in it, and then he had become her life. He seized her and held her with just a stare of his eyes, and she wished for nothing more. The few square meters in which they lived – his room in a communal apartment – the sight of the big city, Moscow, outside the window, a lamp, a telephone, a couch, whitewashed walls, a stone floor, was enough when he smiled. The hurried whispers of neighbors, the running water – the plumbing works after all – the laughter, his friends, colleagues, vodka on the table, her dangerous poetry. "Be careful, honey. You could be imprisoned for that."

And then one day she said, "Perhaps we should leave, everyone is running away."

"I can't, Kate. I'm working on a project. People need me."

"You're choosing 'people' over me?"

"It's my work."

"It's my life."

Kate wished he had a balcony. At that moment she would have thrown herself off it onto the ground into the paradise of nothingness. He held her tight. "Darling, the plumbing is working. What's the trouble?"

She was ignored. "You've made up your mind, I've made up mine." She ended the discussion.

At Sheremetyevo Airport after Sergei had left, she walked through customs into foreign territory, where she stood like a solitary outpost and cried. There was no way back.

"Oh, for heaven's sake," Kate exclaimed, exasperated. "All these cars! Where are they going to? What are they doing here, squeezing me, making me push on the brakes all the time? Perhaps they're also rushing to pay the price for mistakes they have made." Raindrops started fogging the front window, so she turned on the wipers. "And do I need all this rain? Actually, it does not matter. Sun, rain, no one is moving anyways. I'm stuck." She was trying to imagine how he looked now. Had he aged? Had he matured? Is he bald, is he fat? And how will he see her? The way he remembered if he did? Did he ever even think of her? He didn't ask to see her. The meeting would be so awkward – to her, at least. She was making an idiot of herself. She didn't care. She needed to smell him. "Hurry up, stupid cars!" Helpless, she started honking. She glanced at her watch – almost 12 noon – so she had been bitterly pushing on her gas pedal for about two hours. He will be at the airport for another hour and a half, and if a miracle occurs and all these cars will disappear, she would make it on time. She imagined his strong embrace, his mustache against her lips, music softly playing at the bar, and the bartender polishing the glass counter, smiling. And the server would think of his wife to whom he has not said anything pleasant for a long time.

The rain stopped, the cars picked up speed, and the road cleared. Kate's husband would return from his trip today, and she had been thinking of making bouillabaisse, his favorite dish. "Okay," she thought, "so I need to remember to buy tarragon, fennel, basil, saffron of course, make orange peels. It's a good thing I purchased shrimps, fish, mussels, and clams yesterday. And of course I need crusty bread and butter and…" Kate did not notice how she had reached the exit to JFK Airport. "Oh, and I should buy wine. My all-knowing husband loves Chardonnay, so Chardonnay it will be." She exited the highway feeling a surge of energy. "And for dessert, I will roast pears in syrup with a drop of cognac." She made a sharp U-turn and hurried home.

A Late Night Visit

Alik

They clinked tall champagne glasses. "To you," said Alik softly. "Thank you for being with me all these twenty years. It must not have been easy," he chuckled, "but I loved it." They drank half and placed the glasses back on the table covered with a white tablecloth. The band started playing "The Way You Look Tonight." "Would you like to dance?" Alik touched Lida's fingers. Manhattan's symphony of lights burst into the Rainbow Room that was shimmering with crystals, and Lida in her husband's embrace, bewitched by the lights, felt an endless joy being with him here, alive, dancing. He steered her seamlessly–this willowed yoga man—as if she were a luxury car. He was barely touching her and yet in control.

"I just wonder," Lida raised her voice over the high volume of the music, "how could you afford all of this? What's the secret?"

Alik vibrated with excitement that he was trying to restrain. He had borrowed the money from an acquaintance. "It is a secret, darling, so I cannot tell you."

"But I see that you want to, plus there shouldn't be any secrets between us. That reminds me, did you talk to Bella?"

"Bella? Our daughter Bella?" Alik stopped dancing. "What? Did something happen?"

"Ha! Why should I tell you?"

"Is it a secret?" Alik followed his wife back to their table.

"Maybe," Lida laughed. "Look, our food is coming. Bella is fine. No secrets there. She got an A on her paper about 'The Social and Cultural Impact of Movie Media,' that's all."

"I would be curious to read it," said Alik distractedly. In his mind he was debating whether to share with his wife the thoughts he kept in a dark corner of his consciousness, as well as something else. He was wondering what those thoughts would sound like if he ever were to give them a voice. But he never would; he kept them to himself.

Hidden in the inner pocket of his jacket were two white envelopes. Just thinking of their contents sent him into a frenzy of panic. When twenty years ago their daughter Bella had been born, Alik accepted her as a gift from the gods. He was then forty-five, divorced, already had a daughter from a previous marriage with whom he had never managed to establish a relationship. A distant cacophony of reasons and arguments by his first wife muffled with time. But the fact remained. He was alone and lonely until he had met Lida. She had brought meaning to his life and Bella—a nugget of joy, sweetness, and good looks. Emerging through the chaos of Perestroika, emigration, uncertainties, Bella nonetheless had grown into a radiant beauty with a positive outlook on life. At present, a student at NYU Film School, she gravitated to her father, who had been an important documentary filmmaker back in the Soviet Union. They had that in common. Yet he had always thrown sideways glances at her, thinking she was nothing like him, a moody Quasimodo. It was a wacky thought, but he wondered, "Is she really mine, this stunning optimist? Or did Lida, so young at the time of our meeting, experiment with someone else whose seed penetrated her and rooted with enthusiasm? Why did she suddenly agree to marry me so quickly when she had seemed at first ambivalent?" His inner voice had whispered these doubts for years, and they had turned into unanswerable questions.

One of the envelopes in Alik's inner pocket contained the result of a DNA test taken from two cigarette butts, one Bella's, the other one his.

Was he her biological father? He had raised her, guarded her like a treasure, loved her, but still … The other envelope had an answer to his proposal to make a documentary about life in the USSR from after World War II to 1995—two years short of his and his family's emigration to the West. He knew the subject matter all too well and was dying to tell the story to the world. He dreamed of working with Lida as his assistant again, as she had been in the Soviet Union, and to end her misery as an inexperienced manicurist at a nail salon where she was losing her sense of humor. He did not want to think about his own situation as a taxicab driver at the age of sixty-four. Alik had not opened either envelope just yet.

Lida

Alik made a sharp turn, cursed, then apologized, saying that as a driver he was not yet experienced, and drove onto the quay. The Moscow River lay like a black basin with the moon shimmering inside. Straightening the car, Alik said, "They're a wonderful family, closeknit, friendly. You'll see."

"Isn't it late?" asked Lida, her Egyptian eyes outlined in thick black eye pencil shining in the dark.

"At 11 at night? Late?" Alik broke out laughing in a theatrical manner, "Ha-ha-ha." He stopped his brand-new automobile, a Zhiguli, near a tall gray building, at the sight of which Lida thought *some people know how to live!*

On the other side of the Moscow river, like an unattainable dream, the Hotel Ukraina sparkled with a multitude of lights. "You can get out here, Mademoiselle," said Alik still maintaining a sarcastic smile on his thin, wrinkled face. Lida thought that when Alik smiled, his mouth stretched, and he resembled a toad. Having entered the building, she went towards the elevator. "No, no!" Alik exclaimed. "We only have to go to the third floor. Let's take the stairs." Lida made a wry face. Her feet in high heels hurt, and in general she wanted to sleep. "You young people are so weak," said Alik, skipping over two or three steps with his long, thin legs. "Not like us old people, who are fresh as a cucumber at 45. You need to do yoga. Yoga!" He pointed his bony finger at the ceiling.

Lida, breathing heavily, dragged herself up to the third-floor landing and stood next to Alik who was drumming his fingers on the door, merrily yelling, "Open, open, Lev Ivanovich! It's your friends!"

Lev Ivanovich fiddled with the lock for a long time and finally opened the door. "Oh, Alik! What an unexpected joy! With God's blessing. Come in, and the young lady too. A beauty! What's her name?"

"Lida," said Alic and added with irony, "my fiancée."

"Lord, what happiness! Follow me, dear ones," cooed Lev Ivanovich, stepping out of the dark entryway into the depths of the apartment, through the drying diapers hanging on laundry rope in the kitchen where half-empty bottles of baby milk, pacifiers, and open cereal boxes were strewn on a large wooden table. The stove was piled with burned pots and pans, the sink with unwashed dishes. They went into the living room furnished with a couch and armchairs, coffee table, and Yugoslav wall unit—all of which were marks of a good fortune. The armchairs were covered with baby clothes; on the couch lay a fat baby making faces. Over him bent his mother with disheveled hair and sweat stains under the arms of a shapeless sweater.

"Shura, Shurochka! Stop fussing with the baby. Put him to sleep. We have guests. Put delicacies on the table, and I will run to the Hotel Ukraina to get dessert. I'll be back in a second." Lev Ivanovich momentarily disappeared.

Shura looked Lida over from head to toe, then smiled at Alik. "Good evening, Mister Celebrity. To what do we ordinary beings owe this honor?"

"I bought a car," laughed Alik. "We need to mark the occasion. With whom else if not with you!"

Lida looked at him, "Celebrity?"

"Well yes," Shura smiled again at Alik. "To win the first prize at the international film festival is not a small thing. Lev Ivanovich and I are very proud of you, Alik."

"Thanks." Alik turned to Lida, "It's nothing special, a documentary film about the life of the country. I just created a new format. The screen is divided into many squares. In each square runs a different story. In one about a famous dairymaid, in another about a joiner etc., and all the stories intertwine creating a documented presentation of how the country is on its way to constructing communism." Lida wanted to say, "Bullshit" but with tightened lips, said nothing. The baby started to whine. "You're a good boy, I see you will be a film director like me," Alik chirped.

"Or a director of an auto-parts store for Zhiguli cars, like his papa. Without knowing my husband, people should not even attempt to own cars," laughed Shura. "Well, please sit down for a minute. I'll put Misha to bed and return. We'll drink, eat, celebrate your prize, Alik. Did you come directly from the presentation of the new Antonioni movie? Lucky youngsters." With one hand she picked up her son, with the other the baby clothes, and left the room, loudly shutting the door.

"Well, Lida, did you decide to finally give me a kiss? I've been begging before," asked Alik, his voice mocking, as he made himself comfortable on the couch. "After all, I'm taking you to all these showings of foreign movies to which only the elite are allowed." He picked up a newspaper that was laying at his feet and stared at it.

Lida turned to the window, behind which pitch darkness reigned. And although the window was open, no sound could be heard. Perhaps it looked into a courtyard. Lida desperately wanted to see stars instead of nothingness. It was stuffy in the room, hard to breathe. Lida thought that if it was determined for her to die in that moment, she would never have known love—real earthly all-encompassing love like she had read about in novels and seen in all those fantastic films Alik had taken her to …love of which she dreamed, and which she hoped was waiting for her around the corner, if not today, then tomorrow. But the day would come and go and then the next, and there was still the emptiness that had been shadowing her nineteen years of life. Lida unbearably wanted to cry.

"And what did I find in you?" sighed Alik from the couch. "There are such beauties walking at Mosfilm, while I'm with you wasting time — except for your unusual hair, you're kind of plain. And you don't even kiss me, not to speak of anything else. Am I really so repulsive?"

"Alik, how is your daughter?" asked Shura excitedly rushing back into the room alone and purposely avoiding looking at Lida. "How old is she now? Twenty? More, less?"

"Twenty-three," Alik defiantly answered and thought *what a bitch*.

Noisily Lev Ivanovich burst in carrying packages. "For any other person, everything is closed, there's nothing to be had. But for me, the doors open instantaneously, as if by a magic wand." He chuckled, waving his elbow. "Everyone needs auto-parts, whether they have a car or not. And I am the king of that. People are funny." His smile fell from his face as he surveyed the room. "Why are you all sitting here like aliens and not at the table? No one is drinking, eating. Shura!"

"We were waiting for you, Lev Ivanovich," answered Shura haughtily. She opened the doors to the dining room and gestured for them to enter. The dining room like the living room was decorated with dark heavy and Czech crystalware of different colors, both popular among the elite. The chandelier over the table burned with many lights, about which the master of the house immediately complained, "My eyes hurt," he said, and dimming the light, added, "I'm not as vibrant as I used to be. The years are passing. We're not as young as we were, we're aging."

Alik burst out laughing, "What years, Lev Ivanovich? What are you complaining about? How old are you?"

Lev Ivanovich took three bottles of cognac, two lemons, and two boxes with cakes out of a bag. "Shura," he said with concern, "bring shot glasses, plates, a bottle opener, forks, knives." Squinting at Alik, he said, "How old, you want to know? Why, I'm ashamed to say it in front of your bride. Thirty-eight."

An old man flashed through Lida's mind.

Still young, the bastard, thought Alik with envy.

The dining room chandelier hung low casting the table in rose tones like a festive island in the otherwise ghostly desert. The large mirror on one of the walls sparkled with flashes of moving heads and arms pouring liquor and offering plates with various foods, mostly cold cuts. It was reasonably quiet at the table, except for Lev Ivanovich's brusque "Please eat, dear guests" or "Let's drink to you, Alik, and your achievements." He nodded at Lida, "Look what an exceptional girl you got yourself. Lucky but deserved." Lev Ivanovich loudly emptied his shot glass and smacked his lips. "So what does Lida do with her time?" he addressed no one in particular, while examining a label on one of the cognac bottles.

"Lida?" Alik passed a small cracker thickly smothered with black caviar into his mouth. "She grows hair. Look at her. One would think that two heads are needed for that amount of hair." Everyone laughed at the joke, Shura louder than the two men.

Lida tossed the fiery red ringlets of her hair, stood up, and asked where the bathroom was.

"I'll take you." Lev Ivanovich quickly jumped to her side like a young deer. "It's a big apartment. You could get lost. The corridor itself is twelve meters." He gestured to her to follow him. At the end of a long dark corridor like those in Soviet administrative buildings, he gallantly opened the door for her to enter. As she did so, he immediately squeezed behind her and bolted the door. "It won't take long," he whispered, sending a cloud of cognac into her shocked face. She heard the sound of a zipper opening on the level of her thigh. Later, she remembered that he was wearing khaki pants.

"No!" she screamed through her sudden sweat.

He slapped her mouth. "Shut up, beauty, or I'll tell them you seduced me."

He lifted her onto something cold like granite, probably a sink, water dripping nearby. She couldn't breathe …Everything happened in absolute silence except for Lev Ivanovich's heavy sniffing. Having finished, he returned Lida back to the floor. "A cigarette?" he offered flirtatiously.

After Alik and Lida left their host and hostess and were already in the car, Alik moaned plaintively, "When will you finally kiss me? I'm not even asking for anything else. I understand we've just recently met, and you have to get used to me. And you're so young and innocent. Just a kiss, stubborn girl. Just one kiss …"

With dry eyes, through the car window Lida was staring at the mystic yellow moon that suddenly reappeared in the otherwise dark sky. She was slightly worried that the sudden blood in her panties might leak on the beautiful fabric of the brand-new car.

Alik and Lida

"A little more wine?" Alik was already pouring drinks into their two glasses.

"Okay." Lida looked straight at him. "What are we drinking to? Secrets? Or the absence of them? You didn't answer my question before. Do you have any secrets from me?" She raised her glass and her eyebrow.

"Technically"— Alik exaggerated the word — "technically I don't. Would you excuse me, dear. I'll be right back. He got up and walked out of the room.

He suddenly knew exactly what to do. In a black tiled bathroom mixed with dark mirrors, his multiplied reflection brought out two envelopes from his inner pocket. He watched how his multiple hands tore one of the envelopes into small pieces, threw them into the toilet, and flushed. The contents of the other envelope opened and carefully examined brought multitudes of "Yes, yes, yes …" Collectively with the reflections, Alik was the prime witness of this assembly. He walked out from darkness into light thinking that it was too bad that he recently quit smoking. A cigarette would have helped at the moment to balance his emotions. He sighed.

Lida had not touched her favorite walnut-raisin strudel with a scoop of vanilla ice cream dessert. He found her gazing at him curiously. Alik handed her the envelope he was holding. Lida was wearing an elegant black blouse that sparkled from the light of the candles on the table. "What is it?" Lida had learned to be cautious with surprises.

"Just open it."

Lida took the letter out of the envelope and read it. A Mona Lisa smile crossed her face. "Is this your secret?" Her eyes shone.

"This was my secret. It's a present for you."

"Then I will disclose my secret."

"Oh, so you do have one." Alik held his breath, his heart skipped a bit. He was not sure he liked this game anymore. Lida's features were like the surface of the sea on a calm day.

She was not in a rush, carefully observing her husband as if she was seeing him for the first time. Finally her lips parted. "I love you, Baldy."

To Alik her response felt as if a surgeon had just pulled the last stitch through an open-heart surgery and pronounced, "You will live."

Relatives

The swing creaked like fresh snow under the feet. Galya swayed up in the air and back, up and down, heart filled with love, her worries gone, because tomorrow Andrei will marry her. She felt happy and light even with her six-month protruding belly and the rest of her body swollen and heavy. "Liquid-retained," the doctor had said.

Andrei had told her, "I will build a mansion for you. My queen you will be. And the little one," he nodded to Galya's belly, "will become a princess." They hoped for a girl.

Galya decided to rest a bit, to gather energy before going back home, heavy bags with groceries in each arm – a trip to a supermarket after a long day of work cleaning people's teeth, some of which were pretty disgusting, though the pay was good. And yes, they needed the money. Andrei tried as much as he could selling "equipment for doctors," but it was tough, he told her. Once he brought her a bracelet. "Look, honey, I hope you like it. It's costume jewelry for now, soon you'll be dripping in diamonds. Just be patient."

Recently he had moved in with her. "I'll pay half of the bills," he had said, kissing her all over.

She enthusiastically shook her head. "It's very generous of you, but not now. Later, when we're married." It seemed to her that he was secretly relieved. She was thinking about tomorrow, the day they had decided to finally register their marriage. *It's quite all right that it will be just him and me and a baby on the way. What could be better?* She smiled, she was not into big weddings anyway. Her good mood spilled over to a pale young woman sitting on a swing next to Galya's. "Why so sad? Did something happen? Can I help?" Galya felt generous.

"No, thank you," the young woman quietly pronounced and jumped off the swing. Her mouth in a spasm, she vomited right there. Galya noticed that there wasn't any food in what she threw up, just yellow liquid foaming at the edges. The young woman became even paler. "I'm so, so sorry."

"Don't be, sweetheart." Galya witnessed a flood of tears coming down the young woman's face. "Pregnant?" Galya guessed.

The young woman nodded her head, then looked at Galya, her eyes still wet. "But he loves me. He will marry me. He promised."

There was such begging for understanding and belief in her lamenting that Galya stretched out her arm and embraced the young woman. "How old are you?"

"Nineteen," the young woman closed her eyes. "He will marry me," she repeated.

"Of course he will." Galya held the young woman even tighter. "What's your name?"

"Tonya." Tonya looked directly at Galya. "You're pregnant too. We both are."

For some reason they found this funny, and both started laughing. Galya pulled out a handkerchief and wiped Tonya's tears. "When did you move here? I haven't seen you before." Galya checked her wet handkerchief. "Not even a dot of mascara. You're so young, you don't need any makeup to look beautiful. Lucky. I'm almost thirty. My name is Galya, by the way."

"So nice to meet you, Galya. You're so friendly and kind. And pretty. You remind me of my older sister."

"Oh, where are you from?"

"Arizona. My whole family is there. I came here to Florida to make something of myself."

"Oh? Something like what?"

"Like a dancer."

"Swell. And what are you doing now?"

"I dance. I mean, I'm a Zumba instructor. But that's for now. I want to become a real dancer like Taylor Swift." Tonya's eyes sparkled with hope.

"But Taylor Swift is a singer."

"I know." Tonya looked down. "I will learn how to sing. Maybe…" She questioningly glanced at Galya.

"You will, you will, honey. But now you have to take care of yourself, being pregnant and all. Maybe you should think about informing your family. They might want to come here and help."

"Oh no, I can't do that. Besides, Andrei, my boyfriend, will take care of me. He doesn't know yet, but he is so nice and so in love with me. I'm waiting for him here to tell him. And he is tall and handsome." She added dreamily, "With blue eyes."

"Handsome? You said handsome? His name is Andrei?" Tonya noted Galya's sudden pricked up posture. "He lives here?" Galya moistened her lips.

"Yes," Tonya said. "With his mom. He showed me the building a few times, so I decided to surprise him."

"Do you know his apartment number?" Galya became white.

"No, I don't. But it doesn't matter. I'll just wait till he shows up. He works at some sort of office doing something important. I'm not posing too many questions. I don't want him to think I'm a leech. How late can he be? I'll just wait. Is it six or seven already? I forgot my watch." It was still light. The evening did not bring any relief from the heat and humidity. Not a whiff of wind. "I'm sweating," Tonya complained. "It's far from the water, but the rent is cheaper in this area…I live nearby. Andrei and I met at the gym."

At this moment the front door of the building smashed open. And with an awkward gait, Andrei came out led by two policemen. His hands were cuffed. His contorted features indicated that he was quite uncomfortable. He raised his head and saw the two women staring at him, their mouths open in disbelief.

Galya took hold of herself first. "Truly amazing," she hollered. "Hey, officer, could you please tell me what he has done?"

The officer, highly respectful of women's pregnancies – his own wife had not been able to conceive for a long time – said, "Who is he to you?"

"He's my husband," Galya barked.

Tonya felt a bitter taste in her mouth, and a sudden self-pity made her active. "What?! No, she's lying. He's *my* husband-to-be. They're not married."

The officer said, "Then I can't tell anything to any of you."

The three men passed the women. Andrei winked at them. "Drugs," murmured the second policeman, younger and less experienced. They pushed Andrei into the back of a police car. One of the officers got into the driver's seat and turned on the ignition, the wheels screeched against the gravel, and the car shot off.

The two women stood in silence for some time. Galya looked accusingly at Tonya's fragile figure and said "At least he doesn't drink" as if removing the sin of drunkenness would make others appear palatable.

About The Author

Regine Rayevsky Fisher was born in Moscow, U.S.S.R., where she received the equivalent of a Bachelor of Arts degrees in both music and literature. Upon emigrating to the United States, she entered Columbia University's School of the Arts Writing Program, receiving an M.F.A. in 1993. She began to write in English in the late 1980's and has written plays, poetry, song lyrics, and short stories. Regine has taught piano, voice, and Russian language and literature, including most recently at the University of Miami. She has been published in various literary magazines, and one of her short stories won an award from Columbia University that led to her reading it at the KGB Club in downtown New York. Her latest work consists of a collection of short stories in two volumes entitled Dance Me to the End of Love. She lives in Miami with her husband, children, and a small dog named Gemma.

Acknowledgements

I am grateful to my teachers at Columbia University, especially Mary Gordon and Joseph Brodsky for their inspiration and to Maureen Howard who flattered me by comparing my work to that of Kundera and Berberova.

My friends and colleagues both in my Writing Group and outside it kindly read through many of the stories. Deborah DeNicola did an excellent job of editing the volume.

My special thanks to my husband Wesley A. Fisher, my first reader and editorial assistant; to my children Max and Katya for their encouragement and faith in me; to my mother who led the family out of the Soviet Union; and to my father for believing in me.

And then there is my grandson Sam who asks me to get him a cat from Mars.

Other Works

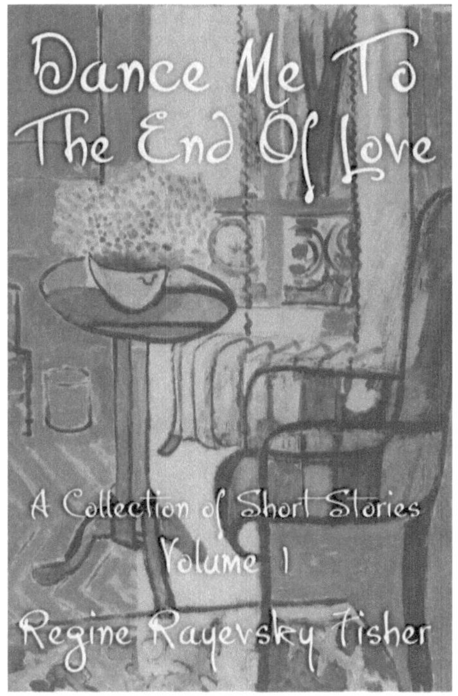

Look for Volume 1 of Regine Rayevsky Fisher's short story collection, *Dance Me To The End Of Love.*

9 781956 271225